Under Saturn's Gaze

Under Saturn's Gaze

Illuminating the Hermit's Lantern Beyond Apocrypha and Oracles

By
ALEJANDRO CASAS

RESOURCE *Publications* · Eugene, Oregon

UNDER SATURN'S GAZE
Illuminating the Hermit's Lantern Beyond Apocrypha and Oracles

Resource Publications
An Imprint of Wipf and Stock Publishers
199 W. 8th Ave., Suite 3
Eugene, OR 97401

www.wipfandstock.com

PAPERBACK ISBN: 979-8-3852-5316-6
HARDCOVER ISBN: 979-8-3852-5317-3
EBOOK ISBN: 979-8-3852-5318-0

VERSION NUMBER 06/05/25

Dedicado a mi papá,
Rolando Santiago Casas Meymije

Contents

List of Figures

Note on figures: Figures 1 and 2 are sourced from Wikimedia Commons and are in the public domain. Figures 3, 4, 5, and 6 are computer-generated images created using ChatGPT's image generation tools. Figure 7 is my own composition, incorporating public domain materials from Wikimedia Commons. Figure 8 is included with the express permission of Ms. Sylvia de Ayala, owner and developer of the website carta-natal.es. Figure 9 is a photograph by David Eucaristía, obtained from Pexels.com and used in accordance with Pexels' free-use license.

ħ

ᴅ

THE BLACK CUBE

The Black Cube

Energy and Matter intertwined, while Mass into light
is refined, and as $E=mc^2$ were defined. In Contrast to
Quantum Contingency and Uncertainty that through
$\Delta x \Delta p \geq \hbar/2$ had materialized, but in Entanglement as
$(i\gamma^\mu \partial\mu - m)\ \psi = 0$ unified. And all the while, in duality
they behave, for as Particles Oscillate and/or Waves
Resonate, it was thus $i\hbar\ \partial/\partial t\ \psi = (-\ \hbar 2/2m\ \nabla^2 + V)\ \psi$

codified. And so it was, in Geometry its Curvature as
$F = dA + A \wedge A$, Graphed, and Traced; meanwhile,
all Dimensions are interlaced, and its Symmetries as
$\dim(\ker DE) - \dim(\operatorname{coker} DE) = \int M\ ch(E) \wedge Td(M)$ cast.
Gravity Space-time bends, $R\mu\nu - 1/2Rg\mu\nu = 8\pi G/c^4\ T\mu\nu$
about a center from a Singularity's end, $T = \hbar c^3/8\pi GMk$.
Where the Cosmic forces blend $(i\gamma^\mu \partial\mu - m)\psi = 0$, and an

Infinity of Boundaries $\int M\ \omega = \int \partial M\ \omega$ are eventually erased.
And so, through Mathematics and Physics often chased,
since it is said, that through their materialist Universe's
Unified Equation the Infinite is closely embraced. But that
are actually through art, science and rhyme demystified.
For it is as Saturn willed it, the Transcendence Source,
Eternally enclosed, in The Black Cube of Space and Time.

DIVINE SINGULARITY

"Self-knowledge reveals to the soul that its natural motion is not, if uninterrupted, in a straight line, but circular, as around some inner object, about a center, the point to which it owes its origin. (V-8-1)"[1]

— Plotinus, The Enneads

1. Plotinus, *The Six Enneads*, V.8.1.

Divine Singularity

Torrents of veiled illusions lifted
through golden rays of illumination,
but first, total darkness was imposed.
And yet, there laid in the middle of it
all a sphere, dark, but glowing in its
Darkness, in deep contrast to the void.

For there it stood, as if floating, detached,
and lonely, but as an equally coherent and
integral part of that primordial cosmic void.
Yet, it was smoother than the other Darkness,
and flowed as if made of liquid or glass, but
Solid, and Perfect in its oneness contained.

Suddenly stopped and stooped by the
levity felt by its pull on my body, the
contrast between it and the background
Darkness became more pronounced. For
it was as if by optical illusion that this
glorious Monad had kept the other
primordial Darkness at bay in the Abyss.

Yet, I am still not able to tell you if it kept
me safe from it in its mercy, by repelling
or keeping it at a distance around me, for
the *other* felt constricting and devouring,
while I was protected in its absolute Grace.

A spark of incandescent light followed,
and an iridescent shallow flame enfolded it
on the two dimensional borders of the sphere.
Radiating in power as if from behind or inside
its core. Resembling in its nature either to a
solar Eclipse or Saturn's esoteric Black Sun.

A series of sounds chased right after, like
echoes of words in water that gave way to a
rapid, short and forceful flow of vibrations,
abruptly squelched by a burst of successive
and even more terrifying, pressurized sounds
of rapture .Willfully holding on, trying to
withstand and decipher, the words behind
the ruptures of such powerful sounds, a
sensation of overwhelming Fear overcame me.

Barely holding on, and looming on the cusp
of being overwhelmed by its *numen*, I was
forced to let go and bask in its sovereignty.
And It was only then so, that fear gave way
to delight, and control dissipated to a luminous
safety net of faith that encapsulated my body
as the reverberating vibrations of healing sounds,
while uplifting it until it was lying horizontally.

Unexpectedly, while inside this node of ecstasy,
That seemed to be using my body as its axis, rays
of light shot from the ignited flame surrounding it
and entered it at curved angles while forming a
golden spiral grid in the background Darkness.
A *matrix* of expanding and contracting curvilinear
rays that are continually transformed and sealed
while progressively evolving and developing anew.

Beautifying it as a skilled artisan raises a fragile
and riven clay pot into a kintsugi vessel. Expanding
and molding my intuitive understanding into a
crucible of desperately sought peace and wisdom,
reforged into a blessing of certainty in discovering,
it's act as a cosmic interplay between the primordial
trinity of the progenitive architect and the entangled
primeval antitrinity of the devouring chaos beasts.

Overcome and burdened by this undeserved gift of
Illumination that was far above anything ever
expected, for it stretched out beyond any reason
and mapped its teleology, but in a flash so fast
that I was barely able to track and count it
It came first as numbers and motion, second
as the linear Progression and evolution of life.

In its powerful simplicity, it is understood.
All life its one, and all oneness in life
Is expanded, made aware and returned.
And so, from this niche surrounded by
The Primordial Darkness, did the living
Universe and its Laws come forth. And
beyond Him, my mystical sight did not go.

The Word

Spark.
First light.
Then sound.
Like, singing of Tibetan bowls.
Silence follows.
Then loud and forceful pressure.
Like, a chant of Tibetan horns.
Smoothed right after, by
AAAAUUUUMMMM; reverberates.
Calming vibrations, rapture.
AAAAUUUUMMMM; reverberates.
Light overtakes, darkness banishes.
AAAAUUUUMMMM; reverberates.
One or none, exist.
Knowledge channeled,
Wisdom recalled.

The Occult

Sinister

I-Daemon

Oh, you, owner of my dreams!
Oh, you, owner of my susurrated
thoughts and reflections.
You taught me to search
amongst my regrets and
commandments for pearls of
wisdom and diamonds forged
in the pressures of experience.

Yet, they taught me that I am
nothing more than an impediment
to the divine wisdom and will.
So, why bother with growing
pains? Set me free and lead
me on the right Path, to my
destiny. And do not trick me,
for I am your light, that I am.

II-Satan

The wind is blowing, the
clouds are roaring. Time is
flowing, and yet everything
stands still. All is beginning
to happen, as it has happened
before. A wooden house
rises from a uniform slope.
Burning in the mist of a dark

cold forest, like a phosphorous
sun. Blood-red and gold, like
a garden's marigold. From
the darkness stood forth a
silhouette, unrecognizable in
form. An echoing thud is heard,
like that of a metal entering
water, and everything gets

condensed under its pull. The
gravity of the moment swallows
the lightness of the Moor. For
intoxicating Darkness steeped
in fear is the reward. Decay is
vicious and Oblivion is your lot.
So, why must you be reaped for
what you did not sow? *-is asked*

Lucifer Unearthed

The decision had been made for him, first by his mother and father, or perhaps their mothers and fathers. Secondly by the structures outside him and thirdly by the structures inside of him, but ultimately by the mystery of life, that which then theologians and mystics call the hand of god or the forces of nature (universe). The decision had been years in the making, but somehow it still felt novel, like a breath of fresh air. He had packed his belongings, had started the engine, gotten inside his car, but did not know the destiny, or perhaps less romantically, he did not know where he was going.

He pondered: what am I to do with this 2 dollar bill? It is worse for wear, and perhaps there are others that need it. Why do I save it? How did I end up with….. Oh, Yes! I remember, Ignacius, Ignacius gave it to me. In exchange for that rose colored coin. Hahaha, that half-made up chemical concoction.

I will put it in the back of the sunshield, it may come in handy. As for the pistol I will lay it at the feet of my ever present companion, perhaps forgetting for a second his job; like daring him to play a game of Russian roulette. Nah, it would be too easy. Besides, there is no way out of it, like a loaded dice, the bullet always falls to the gambler's debt.

The radio said it was half past 7:00PM, but it seems like an autumn evening or an Indian summer, as they say. The third time I checked the glove compartment I remembered the map, but this time around I am not recalling the town. Wait, what was that movement on the 19th century?

Yes, the eugenics movement. I recall the name of the town being named in that matter. Who knows, maybe I am remembering half-invented truths. The road is heavy, or maybe is the car, who knows, it is always very hard to tell. A good car makes for a good journey, but lacks the gravitas of being focused, while a bad car gives you so much trouble, that you are so focused that you miss out on the scenic route. There is a sign coming up.

St. Eugene
Next exit   15 Miles

Fifteen miles, is that much? I guess it depends. No matter, why do I always waste time with these matters, philosophizing, like a tree which falls in the forest and no one hears it, does it make a sound? I, like the tree in the forest, alone hear my thoughts.

There, destination, journey, journeyman's destiny; man in a journey destined to adjourn in destitute, man.

Why is there always a crowd in the market, I guess we all need that sustenance, mad. I will park the car in the tavern. Tavern? That is an odd word to use. I guess those medieval books impressed more than you thought. One must be careful, we think we steer the boat with conscious intention, but those rock and forces push us, and we have no idea of the tides forming, and where our ideas gain forces from, only obtaining knowledge of them, once into waves they form, battering the sterns of our boat.

Buddhism is a boat you use to cross a river, they say, but once you cross you leave it to the river. Is it like the ship of Theseus? Water molds rocks and moves the earth. Is it?

Here we go again with the talks of transhumanism and the unleashing of power. I got to listen to this.

Orator: The future my dear friends, is genetic design. We need our future offspring to live longer, to last longer (youthfully), to be stronger and to surpass A.I intellectually, or A.I will surpass us, and supplants us my friends. We see it already, those hybrids, and those half-pure blood sinners that augment with A.I to keep up. You know these men, you live among them, but they are not your friends. Is this our new Neo-Darwinism, man-machine or machine man. No! By God, No!

What we need are machine less men and women, men and women of pure stock, but unleashed to the full potential of man; the unbound man, the true modern Promethean creation, not these Frankenstein monsters of artificial creation.

Stand with me my brothers and sisters, don't you see, we are at war, and we are losing. We need men and women like these (two specimens pass to the stage where the orator stands lividly) these brothers and sisters, are the future, the transcendental potential in you unleashed. Behold! For you have become immortal, I present you our Providence Inc. ° **Adam** and **Eve**.

"I have had enough of this, these extremists always going against the powers that be; replacing order with chaos to only obtain order and tyranny in new forms. I better rest and eat something; it is already night and there is much to do as of yet. Will I need the pistol? These folk seem like backward people; maybe these reports are unfounded after all. "

"Hello there"

"Yes"

"Judging by the look of your briefcase you seem to be that gentleman that was sent for. What was your name again?"

"Herman"

"Yes, that's right. Herman. Will you be staying long?"

"Only what is necessary. Have you experienced the phenomenon?"

"No, no. Hahaha"

"You seem to be skeptical."

"You know how it is; there are some folks that suffer from an overactive imagination. I you asked me, I'd chalk it up to mass hysteria and boredom, you know. In my day we used to have real problems, now that science has solved much of them, and these folks direct their worries and anxieties aimlessly, darting in the next easiest target, you know."

"So, have you experienced the lights?"

"No, I can't say I have. Hahaha. Even if I wanted to have so fun, I cannot be part of this."

"So, what do you make of the disappearing townsfolk?"

"Well, maybe they had enough of this way of life and left without saying where to, you know. This life is not for everyone, especially nowadays. You know, some people are content with a solitary life, a solid solitude as some say, often however most people are not. Some people just don't want to be found and some don't want to find themselves. Don't you agree?"

"Yes (in fact I do). Would you point me in the right direction of the sightings?"

"Would you point me in the direction of the sightings?"

"Yes of course, if you want to waste your time. Hahahah, Oh God! The woods behind the brewery have been the most consistent location among the stories of the blinding lights. Funny enough, with the full moon and all you will be able to find your way through it. Godspeed my friend, hope you don't catch a cold and become lightheaded. Hahah!"

Herman: Some people sometimes forget their place. It is as if they themselves want to make you lose faith in humanity, by their cynicism and misanthropy. Faith, that's it, isn't it? Faith, or lack of faith, it all comes down to it; all philosophies, all striving and all willing centers on this, faith. And meaning? But words as symbols of things, and words without representations are meaningless, and words with representations have meaning, but if ideas are just ideas of ideas *ad infinitum* and the set of all sets do not contain itself. What then is faith? Is it the understanding? But if we are not able to truly understand, is it an intuition? Like time and space constructed in the threads of language with a center, I. No, is deeper. Trust? No, deeper. Is a fulfillment of the promise of the potential without questioning it. That is faith. Like me, tumbling through these woods, in this thick cold fog, not minding the forest, not minding flora and fauna under this faded light, reflected on that porous looking glass.

Are those people waking aimlessly? Yes, what is it that they have around them, it seems to be gauze; and they are bleeding, or is that tart? Hello, are you with anyone present or are you lost.

Hello! My God! They walk like zombies; I better approach them and see what is what. Hey (as I turn one of them around). What is this, an expressionless face? Is there anyone home? Is like they are stuck in those seconds right after being awaken from a profound sleep and have not focused consciousness, limbo. It is blood! I guess I better let it go; it would not be of much help anyways. There is a pathway just beyond the trench over there. I guess they must have preserved it since the war, as a sort of museum, you know, a memory to the disenfranchised future.

I see a mound just there. What is that I hear? It sounds like…. No it can't be. It is coming from the oak tree; it is massive. The branches are starting to look like rivers when shown from space or like neurons with their dendrite trees. I better check this sound; there may be someone that may enlighten me about these phenomena. It is all very strange, am I dreaming? I don't know anymore. Now, that I get closer I see there is a hole in the body of the tree. Is that an arch in the hole? It looks like it has some inscriptions on it.

Secundum Primum Lustration Factum

Only god knows what it means. There is a stairwell just beyond the hole, a sort spiraling staircase. Bodies started to fall from the top branches, twisting and turning ominously after the cold snap of the robes tightened around their necks; that sound breaking snap, followed by the creaking of the ropes, and the scratching on the branches of the tree. A multiplicity of sounds that become unbearable and nauseating and froze me in place, while staring at their faces and they were soiling themselves, like a macabre chandelier. I must take in faith, the steps into the stairwell, for if there is anything causing these lights and disappearances it must be hiding here.

Will it hold? The ground seems hollow, it moves like its breathing on its own. The stairwell seems to be descending through the roots and ramifications. I can still hear the contortions of the ropes with the alternation of the snapping sound, god that ghostly sound. Was that a flash of light at the bottom of the stairwell (or what seems to be the bottom)? Ahhg, this dirt, is everywhere. If I were to excavate some of the dirt, I may be able to find the source of the light. I sure as hell need it, this darkness is suffocating. There it is, there is the flash again. Wait, is that someone, I see its contour like is standing in front of intense bright light. Yes, it is moving within the densely packed roots and the mass of the mound. Could this be the light that the townsfolk were talking about? However, it is more of a strobing light, about six seconds apart.

Hello! Oh crap, the light has blinded me, it caught me by surprise. There is something moving around me. Whatever it is, it is moving quite rapidly through the roots.

"Hey, can you...."

"Crap! Again, it seems to be leaving a sort of afterimage, impressed on my visual field. God that thing is blinding."

"Can you stop flashing the light, I have..... Damn it!"

"Wait... what is that? (Stuck on the afterimage just developed by the flash of light). It seems some sort of anima, a beast with a gait like a gorilla, but brownish in its coloration. I can hear it borrowing its way through the roots and dirt, like it is the master of this underground maze. Ahhhh!!"

"How ugly, it has a very circular face, unnatural even and small protruding horns on the temples with stripes on them like a goat, with... what is that in the middle, the light is coming from it, it...."

"Ahhh! Damn it!"

"The beast has protruding incisors as well but looks more like a scared animal than it looks dangerous. Why is it acting like is trying to protect something, like a scared animal trying to protect its young from a predator. If I close my eyes quickly, I may be able to see what is emitting the light."

"Ah!"

"Is a third eye! A third eye in the middle of the forehead, between the other two eyes; but it is also highly circular and protruding, dark and muddy or viscous like that of a deep sea fish. I must kill this beast and take it as a trophy to the townsfolk. Bang! Bang! Take that! That damn beast won't die. Bang! Bang! Bang!

Ahh! That god damned blinding light. Am I hitting that damned beast? I believe I am aiming at the afterimage. I must predict its movements and time it well. Bang! There it is, I hear it bellowing like a wounded animal."

"Unnnnn!"

"I killed it! Where is it? I don't see anything. Damn it. What is.... Is a root. Roots and more roots, like a labyrinth, how am I to get out of this. Let me excavate upward. Fuck! Stupid branch, almost split my head in two. I see the moon light. Is that! Is that? Oh Shit, I am stuck. I cannot move. Ummmhh. I see the shape of someone there."

"Hello!"

"It is not moving. Let me try to locate the face. It...it....no, no, no, no, no, no, no! It is me, how can it be, and everywhere. Dead bodies, dead I everywhere on the mound like short grasses trapped in lake ice"

Cipher I

Two tomorrows and one afternoon.
That is what was given and removed.
One evening, zero incantations added.
Three mornings, infinite regressions
subtracted. Four, junctures, free will
Tallied. What is forgiven and what

Is not renewed. What is a preamble,
If not followed in action interpellated
by hebetude? How can it be so? And
when is it just not such? Ceremoniously,
what is, and what isn't simultaneously?
Briars and brambles of beauty and thorns.

A Man Divided

On the way to the country, Shoal Januswort pondered on the impact his visit would have on his hometown. It had been a long time since he had returned from the city. He often considered this a nuance situation as he feared he was no longer the same man. Not only had he changed his tastes and views on life, he would affirm, but he also thought that he no longer recognized his upbringing or who he once was. A lot had happened, he had fallen in love, married, had found "success" in life, and had even been acclaimed and lauded on some occasion; but Shoal had also been heartbroken, had failed, fallen in precarious times, and had even questioned the existence of God. And this, this last point, scared him the most. This moment of honesty or weakness, he often vacillated on its meaning, was the biggest worry of all. It meant an irreconcilable division from his customs and culture, but also his people.

Shoal often also pondered on the meaning of this. Where they still, his people? A question that had often echoed in his head now resounded louder than it ever had.

Shoal's visit was long overdue, and now these existential pangs were but the propulsor for him to visit again. At first, he criticized and even scorned the pace and feel of his hometown village. To him nothing seemed to have changed in the last 13 years. In fact, his memory had failed him and what used to be his entire world during his early formative years, now seemed like a hole in the middle of nowhere. Yet, something was different. He could not tell what was missing at first, but he knew somewhat, someway, his hometown was no longer the same. He desperately searched around for landmarks and buildings to place what he unconsciously understood were missing but could not truly point to.

Nothing was out of place, in fact this was the constant, these things remained the same and was what led him to believe that nothing had changed. Yet, he knew things were not the same.

Was it nostalgia? He pondered, mournfully. No, not that either. It was something more, but also something less conspicuous.

Shoal did not understand. He was not looking for a reason, rather he was looking for a lost feeling and a sensation of home, and an understanding he had lost a long time ago. It was this feeling, which he gained through his hometown and its people, which he was now in search for. Yet, he did not know this, nor could he now attain it. Most of the people he grew up with had also left for the city, and those who raised them were either dead or no longer interested. They interpreted his long absence as abandonment, and now his return was actively ignored as inconsequential. Shoal knew this, yet he did not try to remedy the situation. Instead, he was lost in a world of his own making and was blinded by his selfish pursuit of finding home and understanding his own heart.

Either way no one cares, not even Shoal. Not even the animals seemed to recognize him. He was now a stranger in his own land. An outsider both in the village and in the city. An outsider both to others and to himself. Shoal was poor and yet rich, rich but yet poor. Shoal was a paradox and a paragon of the migrant experience. Shoal was lucky, but also unlucky. Shoal was for others but also for himself. He was a creature divided, with no home and not a well-defined self. Yet he was praised and lauded as the ideal to aspire to at home and far way. Shoal was Shoal, but also that which is much more.

Haunted

Since the beginning of his trips to his friend's house near the caves of Bellamar in Matanzas, Cuba, Eduardo had been haunted by an uneasy feeling of being followed. Sometimes it manifested as fleeting glances, other times as barely perceptible whispers, but invariably he was tormented by a persistent paranoia that he was being watched and called by name. More often than not, Eduardo would not dare to look back or attempt to pinpoint the source of these whispers. Yet, at times, these faint, siren-like calls became so vivid and unsettling that he found himself compelled to glance back or strain his hearing to decipher the murmured words carried by gusts of wind.

Despite these unsettling experiences, Eduardo deeply cherished the open fields, the vibrant conversations with farmers, and the seasoned agricultural workers whose lives intertwined ancestral wisdom with contemporary agricultural practices. They effortlessly blended indigenous and African religious knowledge with folklore, enriching Eduardo's perception of the Cuban countryside. Often, Eduardo would listen to stories of seasons and cycles of life, tales that exceeded his youthful comprehension yet felt mesmerizingly fantastical and magical.

It was within these positive musings and vivid stories that Eduardo sought refuge from his darker moments. Fueled by an intense mixture of fear and excitement, typical of adolescence, Eduardo regularly traveled to his friend Federico's home, carrying his bird cages, ready for their bird-catching adventures. Precocious for his age, Eduardo had already become an integral part of the community, meticulously mapping out and skillfully utilizing prime locations across the countryside for capturing prized birds. He particularly delighted in the meticulous patience required for setting up wooden and bamboo-crafted bird cages equipped with side trap doors, strategically positioned in places he confidently considered ideal.

"Locations no one else knows about," he would proudly exclaim, his youthful voice tinged with pride and excitement.

Eduardo's favorite time for this cherished pastime was winter, when the indigo buntings migrated to the Cuban countryside.

"I love these birds, their color, their presence, and their song," he would frequently share, almost as if reciting a mantra. The farmers and countryfolk who knew Eduardo would often smile warmly at these heartfelt declarations.

"This child has truly made the countryside his home. He knows every road and hidden pathway out here, even those we haven't discovered ourselves. It's as though the Orisha, Kimpungulu, and the nfumbe have embraced him as one of their own," they would remark fondly among themselves after Eduardo departed from their spontaneous gatherings and countryside picnics.

And so, leaving one of these encounters, Eduardo once again headed to his friend Federico's house. Federico, also an avid bird catcher, had become mildly upset with Eduardo lately. He sensed he was gradually losing his friend, who often seemed distant and detached, as if his mind were elsewhere rather than fully engaged in their shared pastime. Federico had raised these concerns with Eduardo before, but Eduardo had always downplayed them, quickly shifting the conversation back to Federico's favorite topic: the painted bunting. Federico adored these birds and often recounted a memorable, yet dubious, sighting near the caves of Bellamar. Everyone suspected it was merely an exaggerated tale, as painted buntings had long vanished from the Matanzas countryside. Nevertheless, they humored Federico, for he was genuinely likable, especially to Eduardo, which was precisely why Eduardo had decided to visit him this particular day.

However, Eduardo himself recognized a shift in his interests and priorities over the past year. Secretly, he had sold much of his cherished bird collection, using the proceeds to buy clothes and jewelry. Moreover, Eduardo now had a girlfriend whom Federico knew nothing about. Since Federico belonged to a different incorporated area of Matanzas, the two longtime friends did not attend the same school. Thus, their weekend rituals continued, but their bond felt increasingly strained.

"So, what's going on with your classes? You still having problems with the Spanish teacher?" Federico asked, trying to break the silence.

"Nah, I just don't pay attention to him anymore. He's a weird little guy who takes himself and literature way too seriously," Eduardo responded unintentionally coldly.

Federico noticed Eduardo's tone and decided not to pursue further questions. A heavy silence followed, which Eduardo eventually recognized, feeling guilty for unintentionally dismissing his friend. His thoughts had simply been elsewhere.

"It's not that I'm not interested, but he only accepts status quo interpretations. The other day, for example, we were discussing Alejo Carpentier's work. He refused to consider that Carpentier's approach to magical realism could also be interpreted as a deeply entrenched European elitist gaze, one that continues to perceive Latin America and the Caribbean through a European imaginary, similar to Edward Said's concept of imaginative geographies," Eduardo exclaimed, surprising even himself with the passion behind his words.

Federico remained silent, unsure of how to respond or what Eduardo was talking about. Increasingly, he noticed his friend erupting into these sudden, angry monologues, which Federico struggled to comprehend. Yet, Federico smiled good-naturedly and joked:

"That guy should go out and spend some time with country folks. Maybe then he'd get his head out of his ass!"

"Hahaha," Eduardo laughed, grateful for Federico's ability to lighten the mood. Eduardo himself had recently noticed feeling angry, confused, and moody, unable to fully grasp why. Internally, he wrestled with conflicting emotions, part of him yearning for his interests and goals to remain unchanged, while another part sought excitement and novelty.

After about an hour of bird catching, Eduardo felt increasingly bored and fabricated an excuse about forgetting groceries his parents had asked him to pick up. He claimed that since he was far away, the bodega would soon close, and he needed to leave promptly. Federico didn't believe him but understood there was no point trying to make him stay.

"For what?" Federico wondered silently to himself.

"He has become almost insufferable. He hasn't even talked about birds or the news that Cristian decided to retire from bird catching and sold his birds. Everyone in the community is buzzing about it and his championship birds! Yet Eduardo hasn't uttered a single word. Maybe I'll try to get Henry to join me to find the painted bunting," Federico childishly strategized internally.

Thus, the friends parted ways, unknowingly concluding what would become their final bird-catching outing together. Although they remained friends into adulthood, their interactions gradually became distant and fragmented, eventually transforming into a complete estrangement. Years later, each failed to recognize in the other the friend of their childhood. Both preferred, without ever explicitly discussing it, to interact as little as possible, hoping to preserve intact their cherished memories of friendship and youthful adventures. These memories became precious internal landscapes, golden moments that they revisited during difficult and burdensome periods of adulthood.

Now, as Eduardo walked back down the mountainous countryside terrain, he began ruminating again on his increasingly extreme shifts in mood, interests, and focus. He felt a pang of guilt for how he'd treated Federico yet simultaneously felt secretly relieved about slowly distancing himself from their shared pastime. Suddenly, paranoia resurfaced; he was certain he heard footsteps and whispers again.

"What is going on? Has someone placed a hex on me? I'm not going crazy; I definitely hear footsteps and the rustling of the wheat stalks in the field," Eduardo argued internally.

He slowed his pace to listen carefully, wanting to discern if the sounds persisted even when he stopped. Abruptly, Eduardo turned around and loudly demanded:

"Who goes there? What do you want?"

No response followed, only the gentle murmurs of birds, the distant caw of a crow, tractors rumbling, barking dogs, bleating sheep, and faint snippets of conversations from farmers near the highway that circled the mountain. Eduardo waved towards them, and they waved back. Yet worryingly, no one else appeared nearby. He continued walking, and so did the mysterious sounds. This troubled him, though he decided to pretend he could no longer hear them.

It was at this moment that Eduardo started reflecting on when these unsettling sensations first began. Retracing his thoughts, he pinpointed their origin to his first visit to his girlfriend's house. Melany had invited him to her family's old colonial home in the city center, and the oldest and busiest part of town. The house was a two-story building, with bedrooms occupying most of the upstairs space. A long, wide staircase connected the floors, and two spacious bedrooms were situated at opposite ends. Melany's parents, Jorge and Jacinta, slept in the bedroom facing the backyard, while Melany's room faced the street. Eduardo had grown familiar with the home over the past year and even assisted Jorge in moving items out of the attic.

While in the attic, Eduardo and Jorge had discovered what appeared to be a makeshift reading corner, featuring old books stacked messily alongside a cleared wooden beam seemingly used as seating. Jorge had been visibly shocked by this discovery, repeatedly exclaiming throughout the following week, especially whenever the topic arose in conversation, which he often sought out with guests and friends, that no one had been up in the attic for years. It was in this attic, Eduardo now remembered, where he had first experienced an oppressive sensation, a cold sweat accompanied by an unsettling feeling of being watched or judged.

By now, Eduardo had reached the base of the mountain. He paused momentarily before heading towards some bushes on the right, about 100 meters away, where he had hidden his bicycle earlier. He sincerely hoped to find it, as two months prior, another bicycle had been stolen, the second one in as many years. Finding his bike was crucial; he eagerly wished to visit Melany and knew that having his bicycle ensured he would reach the city center before nightfall. His anxiety grew as he searched, initially struggling to recall precisely where he had hidden it. The uncertainty intensified his frustration and worry that he might miss seeing Melany on time. His parents enforced a strict rule prohibiting nighttime visits in their bedroom. Frustrated, he cursed aloud:

"Damn it! Where are you, you fucking bike?" he blurted out angrily.

Eduardo felt irate, not just about the missing bicycle, but at himself for his recent absent-mindedness and diminished enthusiasm for life. Few things currently brought him joy, and among them was spending time with Melany.

"Aha! Found you, rusty old piece of scrap!" he triumphantly exclaimed upon finally spotting his bike.

He immediately jumped onto the seat and pedaled as fast as he could, determined and focused.

As Eduardo rode his bicycle toward his girlfriend's house, he passed familiar landmarks and acquaintances, greeting some while inadvertently ignoring others, lost in thought about his persistent feeling of being haunted. He noticed that the faster he pedaled, the less he felt the sensation of being watched. Motivated by this realization, he accelerated his speed further. At one point, lost in thought and riding carelessly, he misjudged the curve of a corner and collided straight into a wall at approximately 15 miles per hour. He had desperately tried to brake, but strangely, the brakes seemed ineffective, as though someone or something had prevented them from gripping the wheels. Although the impact was painful, Eduardo immediately stood up, attempting to act as though nothing had happened. However, some neighborhood boys, whom he'd previously fought in childish gang-style conflicts a few years earlier, had witnessed the incident and wasted no time mocking him.

"Idiot!"

"What happened, forgot how to ride a bike?"

"Need to borrow my sister's training wheels?" they taunted. These insults lingered painfully in Eduardo's mind long after he had left the scene.

He didn't mind their taunts but flipped them off anyway, prompting the group of seven boys to leap from the stairwells of the building, attempting to chase after him. Eduardo, knowing he couldn't take them all on, quickly sped away before they could catch up.

About ten minutes later, nearing Melany's home, Eduardo started to feel pain and numbness in his wrist and left shoulder. Only then did he realize he had instinctively reacted to the fall by placing his right hand in front of his face and arching his left shoulder protectively. These were the areas most impacted by the collision. Fortunately, he hadn't suffered any fractures, just intense pain from contusions. Upon arriving at his girlfriend's house, he called out to her:

"Phwwwwwhht! Melany! Melany! Melany!"

Someone peeked through the window blinds, and after about thirty seconds, Melany swiftly opened the main door and rushed out to greet him. Her eagerness momentarily confused Eduardo, though he didn't dwell on it, distracted by his pain. He winced sharply when Melany embraced him, prompting him to quickly explain his accident. Immediately, she began fussing over him, nursing and comforting him, something Eduardo secretly adored. Indeed, Melany's caring and nurturing nature were among the qualities he cherished most about her, contributing greatly to his affection.

Once inside, Melany quickly informed her parents about Eduardo's accident, prompting their immediate empathy and concern. Over time, they had grown genuinely fond of Eduardo, treating him like the son they had never had, for Melany was their only child.

They sat Eduardo at the table in the entrance area of the living room, conversing with him while Jacinta went searching for the first aid kit. Eduardo had several deep scratches that had bled considerably, something that surprised him as he hadn't initially noticed. He felt a strange sense of numbness and indifference toward his injuries, as though he somehow deserved or needed punishment. This intrusive thought startled him, as he had never before experienced such feelings or ideas.

Eduardo then mentioned to Jorge and Melany that his neck hurt significantly, accompanied by a heavy sensation. Concerned, they suggested it might be whiplash and discussed taking him to the hospital. Jacinta returned and agreed, but first recommended disinfecting his wounds with alcohol to prevent infection. Melany, however, insisted that betadine was superior as an antiseptic. The mention of betadine reminded Eduardo of their time together in organic chemistry class and the silly, childish pun he'd invented there, a semi-rhyming joke that, oddly enough, he still felt quite proud of. In his dazed state, Eduardo decided now was the ideal moment to share it. He'd been holding onto it for a long time, and now it burst forth spontaneously, as if released from a tightly coiled spring:

"*In a daydream benzene as a snake did Kekulé see.*
From its mouth to tail six equivalent bonds aromatically sealed were these.
In resonance, heterocyclically cooked not from snake oil or beta-dine, but from pyridine
As he worked with it in the hood, and then tried to get pyrrole"

—while faintly laughing and pointing at his hand tattoo of Kekulé's benzene ring, with its delocalized 6 π-electrons, as understood in modern molecular theory, inside an Ouroboros.

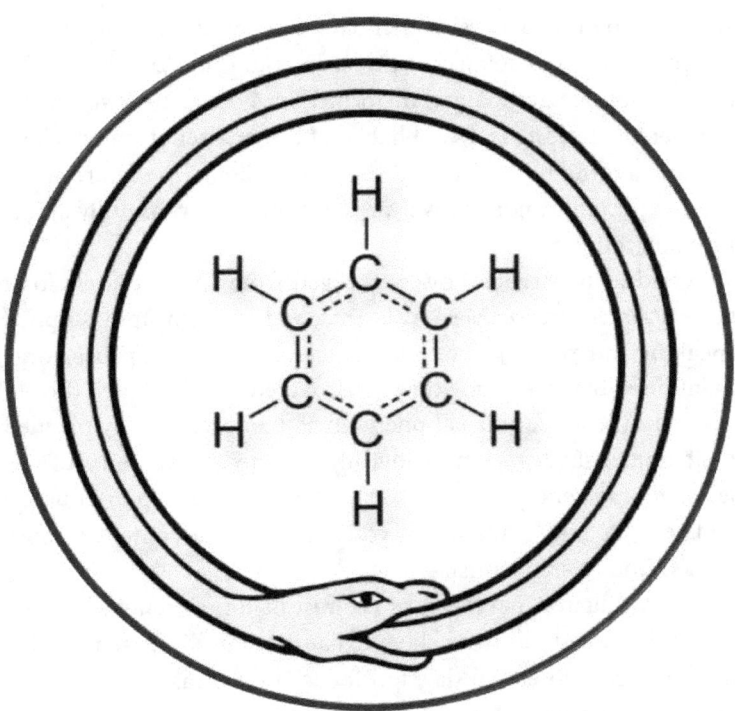

"Idiot! Is this really what you're thinking about right now?" Melany exclaimed, smacking him gently on the back of his head.

Eduardo groaned in response while Jorge laughed heartily, though it was unclear whether his amusement was due to Eduardo's joke or Melany's playful smack on Eduardo's injured head. Jacinta, meanwhile, remained more concerned with Eduardo's wellbeing and anxious about what his parents might say. She began applying the betadine to Eduardo's wounds, causing him to wince sharply in pain, slamming his left hand onto the table and stomping his left foot on the floor. The pain was so intense that Eduardo felt momentarily lightheaded.

It was precisely at this moment that Eduardo first saw it, through the small spaces between Melany, Jorge, and Jacinta's bodies, a black cloud slowly descending the staircase. Eduardo was transfixed, as though the shadowy presence demanded his undivided attention. Meanwhile, Melany, Jorge, and Jacinta continued speaking to him, expressing their concern and the urgency of getting him to the hospital. Yet Eduardo could not look away. The black cloud had gradually transformed into the distinct silhouette of a person, lacking feet, and halted at the first set of stairs, where a small landing turned toward the second floor. The figure stood there expectantly, not passively, but as though purposefully awaiting something.

Suddenly, strange noises emerged from the spandrel closet beneath the staircase. Melany, Jacinta, and Jorge abruptly stopped speaking and exchanged uneasy glances. After a tense pause, Jorge mentioned that ever since they'd discovered and discarded the old books in the attic, unusual phenomena had increasingly plagued their home, shadows appearing, unexplained movements of objects, doors opening spontaneously. Jorge then turned to Eduardo and began to ask, "Eduardo, do you remember the content of those books? They were Flemish—"

But Eduardo never heard the rest of Jorge's sentence, as he suddenly passed out from sheer exhaustion and intense pain. He had neglected to eat all day, too focused on pleasing others and forgetting to care for himself.

~

Weeks later, after Jorge, Jacinta, and Melany had taken Eduardo to the hospital and he had fully recovered, Eduardo returned to their home to visit his girlfriend. He arrived after school with Melany, and her parents invited him to stay overnight, provided his parents agreed. Jorge and Jacinta made a special exception, explaining that it was due to Eduardo's recent ordeal, believing Melany's company could further aid in his recovery. Eduardo was delighted, especially because it was Melany's birthday the next day. When he mentioned this excitedly, they laughed warmly and said:

"We know!" Jorge and Jacinta exclaimed, raising their eyebrows and sharing a playful smirk.

"Good thing you're a good boy and we like you, otherwise, we'd think you're not bright enough for our daughter!" Jorge joked, causing everyone to burst into laughter.

"Hahaha," Eduardo laughed along, mirroring their good-natured humor, though internally he barely registered their playful remarks. He felt deeply excited and slightly anxious about spending his first night with Melany.

Eduardo and Melany spent a relaxed evening in the living room with her parents, watching movies and enjoying board games, a favorite pastime of Jorge's. Throughout the evening, Eduardo and Melany stole glances at each other, exchanging affectionate touches filled with anticipation for their private time together. As midnight approached, Eduardo cleverly suggested stepping out briefly to buy some ice cream for Jacinta and Melany, knowing they both enjoyed it during movie nights. Melany initially objected, reluctant to let him go after spending so much time apart due to Eduardo's hospitalization and recovery. Surprisingly, Jorge supported Eduardo's idea, which puzzled both Melany and Jacinta.

What Melany and Jacinta didn't know was that earlier in the evening; while grilling meat on the barbecue, Eduardo had secretly coordinated with Jorge. Eduardo planned to surprise Melany with additional gifts, chocolates and a teddy bear, beyond the present he had already prepared. He wanted to reward Melany for being such a wonderful and supportive girlfriend.

And so Eduardo stepped out to purchase the chocolates and the teddy bear. He quickly returned and waited in the car until it was nearly midnight, intending to surprise Melany precisely on her birthday. While waiting outside, he decided to lean against Jorge's parked car in front of their house to wait more comfortably. He rested against the side doors facing west, towards their home.

At about 11:40 PM, Eduardo received a text message from Melany asking if he would be much longer, noting it was close to midnight. He replied that he was almost there, still determined to surprise her at exactly twelve. While responding to Melany's message, a drunken neighbor approached Eduardo, asking if he had any cigarettes. Eduardo quickly replied that he did not, but the intoxicated man persisted, rambling about his nighttime exploits, which increasingly irritated Eduardo. To signal that he was occupied and about to go somewhere, Eduardo turned to point toward the house but suddenly froze in shock at what he saw.

Instantly, he stopped listening to the drunk neighbor, who, noticing Eduardo's lack of attention, stormed off angrily, cursing him as he went. Eduardo, however, remained motionless, completely transfixed by the sight in front of him. On the second floor of Melany's home was a balcony outside her room, a familiar spot where they would often sit and stargaze together. But now, standing there, he clearly saw the figure of a young girl. Initially, Eduardo assumed it was Melany, especially given the dim lighting. The only illumination came from a distant streetlamp, creating enough visibility to discern shapes but not precise details. Yet, he quickly realized this figure could not be Melany, as she had platinum blonde hair, whereas Melany was brunette. Additionally, the girl appeared to be around nine or ten years old, heightening Eduardo's unease, as he knew of no family member resembling her.

Feeling deeply unsettled, Eduardo swallowed nervously and called out to the girl:
"Melany. Melany. What are you doing up there?" There was no reply.

"Melany, what are you doing on the balcony at this hour, in the dark? Melany! Why aren't you answering?" he called out more forcefully, increasingly frustrated by the silence.

"What the hell is wrong with people? Why isn't that person answering? Who is she? I can see her clearly. Hey, you in the red jacket!" he shouted, able to see only her torso and face above the balcony's concrete railing.

Still receiving no response, Eduardo grew exasperated. He now noticed with discomfort that the girl appeared to gaze lovingly at him, her chin resting on her hands. She was observing Eduardo intently yet offered no reaction to anything he said or did, until Eduardo pointed directly at her, exclaiming:
"Hey you! Yes, you! What are you doing there? Who are you?"

At this, the girl abruptly stood up, startled, stepping back as if astonished to realize Eduardo could indeed see her. After a brief moment of hesitation, she deliberately lowered herself out of sight, hiding behind the balcony railing.

Eduardo, noticing her disappearance, quickly rushed inside the house, his heart racing in a frenzy. When he entered, he found Melany, Jacinta, and Jorge calmly sitting in the living room, watching the movie, oblivious to the strange scene Eduardo had just witnessed.

"Hey, you're back!" they said in unison as Eduardo entered.

"You brought... what's this? Aww, you bought chocolates and a teddy bear for Melany. How sweet!" Jacinta exclaimed warmly.

Jorge approached Eduardo, gently patting him on the shoulder and winking, but immediately noticed that Eduardo appeared disheveled and pale as a ghost.

"Eduardo, what's wrong?" Jorge asked with concern.

Initially, Eduardo couldn't find his voice.

"Baby, what happened? What's going on?" Melany asked urgently, becoming worried.

They quickly brought him some water, and after calming slightly, Eduardo explained what he'd seen outside. At first, they listened quietly, exchanging puzzled looks, then tried to ease the tension by making light of the situation. As scientists, Melany's parents naturally felt uncomfortable discussing such unusual occurrences. After some reassuring dialogue, they eventually convinced Eduardo, or rather, Eduardo chose to believe, that what he'd witnessed was perhaps a trick of the light, possibly a reflection from the large glass doors leading to the balcony. Though not entirely convinced, Eduardo welcomed the explanation as a comforting lie to soothe his nerves.

Soon enough, midnight arrived, and as the clock chimed twelve, they joyfully celebrated Melany's birthday, momentarily forgetting the troubling event. Around 1 AM, Melany's parents started feeling sleepy and decided to retire to their bedroom after bidding Eduardo and Melany goodnight. The couple lingered downstairs in the living room for another twenty minutes. Then, with a gentle glance and a subtle nod, Melany took Eduardo's left hand and quietly led him upstairs to her room.

Once inside, Melany revealed that she'd obtained a spliff from a classmate and wanted to share the experience with Eduardo. Though Eduardo typically wasn't interested in that kind of thing, he found himself agreeing, perhaps due to his recent craving for excitement and novelty or influenced subconsciously by the unsettling experience he'd had earlier.

They smoked the joint together on Melany's balcony, which inadvertently caused Eduardo's earlier anxiety and paranoia to resurface intensely. Noticing his discomfort, Melany tenderly kissed him, alleviating his fears and anxiety and allowing him to momentarily forget his unease. Eventually, they stepped back into Melany's room, where they became intimate, making love, as Melany preferred to call it.

However, their intimacy was soon interrupted by faint whispers, which initially seemed to come from the television they had switched on at a very low volume to mask their own noises. They paused, straining their ears, and distinctly heard sounds resembling paper tearing, originating from the attic. Loud footsteps, reminiscent of heavy winter or work boots, soon joined these strange noises, greatly unsettling the couple. They stopped entirely, frozen in fear. Melany, visibly frightened, whispered urgently:

"I think we need to tell my parents. There might be someone in the attic."

However, this time it was Eduardo who tried to reassure Melany, suggesting it was merely an effect of the marijuana causing them to imagine things.

"Who could possibly be upstairs?" he reasoned gently. "There's no way anyone could have accessed it, and your family's been home all day."

His words somewhat convinced Melany, and after calming her down, they cautiously continued, though she remained hesitant, periodically interrupting their intimacy with anxious whispers: "Did you hear that?" Eduardo, however, was distracted and paid little attention to these remarks, his mind was elsewhere.

Suddenly, everything changed when the wooden sliding door to the bathroom forcefully and inexplicably slammed open. They both jumped in fright, and Melany screamed loudly. Eduardo quickly tried to calm her, terrified that her parents might find them like this and forbid him from seeing her again. But Melany was inconsolable, and her cries soon woke her parents.

Upon entering the room, Jorge and Jacinta immediately noticed Eduardo and Melany were high, dismissing Eduardo's panicked explanations as drug-induced paranoia. They expressed deep disappointment, instructing Eduardo to gather his things as they would drive him home immediately. Eduardo pleaded with them not to tell his parents, at which point Melany intervened, claiming it had all been her idea. Her parents, however, remained skeptical but ultimately agreed not to inform Eduardo's family. Instead, they simply dropped Eduardo off at home, telling his parents that an urgent work emergency required their immediate attention at the lab.

From then on, Eduardo was not permitted to see Melany outside of school. Nevertheless, they found ways to secretly meet until their parents eventually discovered these encounters and decided to move away. Melany's family exchanged houses with colleagues from another province who had always dreamed of relocating to Matanzas, and shortly after, they left. Eduardo never learned exactly which province Melany's family moved to.

Years later, Eduardo and Melany unexpectedly met again at a party in Varadero, reigniting the passionate connection they'd once shared. This time, as adults, they fully consummated the relationship that had been abruptly interrupted years earlier. As they lay together afterward, Melany suddenly brought up the strange occurrences from that unforgettable night. She confided those unsettling events had continued after Eduardo left, children's laughter echoing through the house, sounds of small feet running around, the distant singing of a woman, the clanking of a mop on the floor, and kitchen cabinets mysteriously opening overnight. Nothing had been quite as dramatic as that evening, she admitted, yet the events remained deeply unsettling.

"As a matter of fact," Melany began, sitting up cross-legged on the bed, "about two years later, we ran into the family we'd exchanged houses with at a company retreat. Listen to this, they told us they couldn't stay in that house longer than a year! They experienced terrifying phenomena too: paper tearing sounds, whispers, and even intense poltergeist activity. Crazy, isn't it?"

"I don't know if 'crazy' is the right word, but yeah," Eduardo responded softly.

"What about you? Did anything similar happen to you afterward?" she asked curiously.

"No, nothing like that. Thankfully, I never experienced anything similar again. Although, I did get baptized a few years later, but that was unrelated," Eduardo replied.

Melany shrugged slightly, and soon the conversation shifted back to affection and their mutual desire to make up for lost time. They never spoke about the incident again for the duration of their relationship, though both carried the vivid memory with them, occasionally resurfacing as an unsettling reminder of their shared past.

Eros

When I look into your eyes,
I wonder, what wonders you
And I! Beauty, curiosity and
passion, they seem to shine.

Yet, what i would give to see
in them not just these and
other common excitements,
but also their love for you and i!

Betrayal

Remembering on things
that have past, i found
myself on the same lake
as that night, night in

which we told each other
of things that would never
come to pass. Nor did i
expected but more than

the promises to fault, for
the lake now seems so
rocky and so empty at

first glance and yet it
feels more beautiful
than i ever really thought.

Hekate

At the early hours of the morning on the first Monday of the first week of the year 2020, Damian woke up panic-stricken at the sound of air horns blaring through his city. Awakening from the stupor of deep-seated rest, he recounted and pondered the significance of these sounds. Half-somnolent, caught between sleep and wakefulness, his subconscious had reinterpreted the air horns as angelic trumpets. This eerie misperception contributed to his distress and profuse sweating, even though it was quite cold and frosty outside. Damian wondered for a moment what could be the cause, perhaps an emergency drill or a sudden onset of severe weather. However, he soon remembered the far graver reality and its peculiar weight: the global COVID-19 pandemic had entered its exponential phase. A communal feeling of fear, insecurity, instability, and pervasive worry now dominated everyday life.

Being quarantined was not easy, but dealing with loss on such a massive scale was even more jarring. Damian had lost his job, friends, school, and the simple joy of the outdoors. Even the once-mundane act of going out to get groceries now seemed like an unprecedented act of bravery. Nature itself felt treacherous and dangerous. He briefly mused about the 16th- and 17th-century explorers and their encounters with untamed and uncharted territories, though this thought quickly gave way to much more serious concerns. A flicker of guilt crossed his mind at what he deemed childish musings in such dire times. Mystified, Damian pondered:

"How can this be part of eternal providence? Is this a divine joke, a test, or just plain cruelty, retribution for humanity's transgressions against nature or God?"

More immediate, however, was the pressure on him and his parents: the looming threat of eviction due to unpaid rent and the unrelenting burden of working frontline service jobs in the midst of a deadly pandemic. So-called "essential workers," once relegated to the fringes of society and treated as third-class citizens, were now suddenly hailed as heroes. Yet, the praise did little to alleviate the hardship. This decision, whether to risk homelessness or exposure to a deadly virus, weighed on Damian like a ton of bricks pressing down on his chest. In the span of a single week, he had suffered two panic attacks, a first for him. Known for his resilience and tolerance for pain and the pressures of survival, Damian was startled by these episodes. Yet, with the options reduced to either suffering panic attacks at home or risking exposure in a hospital, he resigned himself to enduring in silence.

He also did not want to expose the source of his weakness. The mere thought of losing his parents was beyond his comprehension, an unacceptable prospect. He was truly worried, for the first time in his life. He swore to do everything in his power to protect them. At that moment, his inseparable Anatolian Shepherd dog, Braisis, came to greet him. Damian fed him, and for a fleeting moment, he felt a small joy at being able to care for his companion. This moment sparked an epiphany. He needed to act, to take control of his fate. Though he typically preferred to go with the flow and let things fall into place, something within him shifted. A transformation was taking root. At that instant, a line from one of his favorite poets, John Milton, surfaced in his mind:

> "*What in me is dark*
> *Illumine, what is low, raise and support,*
> *That, to the height of this great argument,*
> *I may assert Eternal Providence,*
> *And justify the ways of God to men.*"[1]
>
> —Paradise Lost, Book I, lines 22–26

Now, more than ever, these words resonated with him. They ignited a resolve. Without hesitation, Damian told his parents that he would go out for groceries and reassured them not to worry. He grabbed his mask, wallet, and hoodie and stepped out the door.

1. John Milton, *Paradise Lost*, Book I, lines 22–26.

However, as soon as he turned the corner of his apartment complex, a wave of dizziness overcame him. He felt lightheaded and short of breath. Sitting down to steady himself, he was suddenly overtaken by another intense surge of panic. He lay against the wall, struggling to catch his breath, when, at a distance, he noticed a strange and unsettling sight. He did not know if he was hallucinating, if it was merely a trick of oxygen deprivation, or if it was something far more mystical. He had experienced overwhelming emotions before, but on the opposite end of the spectrum. This, however, was so intensely negative, so utterly overwhelming, that he did not recognize it at first for what it was. Overwhelmed by the sheer intensity of the experience, he did not recognize it for what it was at first.

A black, undulating mass loomed on the horizon, drawing nearer. At first, it seemed like storm clouds and thunder, but as it advanced, it became something far more sinister. An all-consuming, yet eerily cold, black fire with soft white edges spread across the landscape. Damian felt terror unlike any he had ever known. He had experienced overwhelming emotional episodes before, but always on the opposite end of the spectrum. This darkness was something entirely different, something foreign. Soon, the faraway sight of a black, undulating mass on the horizon became clearer and nearer. What first seemed like dark clouds and thunder soon transformed into an all-consuming, yet eerily cold, black fire with soft white edges. It was terrifying for Damian to have such a dark mystical experience, one that stood in sharp contrast to his previous, more pleasant ones.

The black fire appeared to be consuming people from the inside out. It entered their lungs, suffocating them, draining the air from their chests, and burning them from within. One by one, people fell ill, collapsing like dominoes. That was when he noticed something even more unsettling. From within the fire, spirits appeared, as if swimming up and down between the shifting boundaries of the black mass and the physical world, the street, the walls, the doors of buildings. They thrashed desperately, as if trying to escape in vain. Their spectral arms, legs, torsos, and faces twisted in torment, struggling to free themselves, yet bound by some invisible force. The most disturbing part was that although the spirits seemed to be screaming, crying, and voicing their pain and desperation, at most they sounded like a quiet storm of murmurs, muffled by the earth-shattering pulses emanating from the center of the black fire.

These pulses came in intervals of three seconds, and they were so powerful that they corrupted and cracked every structure they touched. They felt like miniature earthquakes, devastating everything in their path. Damian was transfixed by the sheer force and pressure of the pulses, even at a distance. They made him feel ill and wounded in a strange, inexplicable way, as if a wall of sound had crashed into him, bruising him internally. He thought he could taste blood in his mouth. Yet, he did not move. He remained seated, overwhelmed by the immensity of the force and power, as well as the vividness of the vision. However, this soon changed when he noticed three monstrous figures emerging from the center of the black fire. They resembled Wendigos, yet they had no feet. These creatures attacked people on the streets with their long, black fingernails, leaving gaping wounds that they then used to carve out their victims' entrails. It seemed as though they were feeding on the entrails to satiate their hunger while also performing some strange ritual. Behind them, they dragged a retinue of corpses, all strung together by their own innards.

Terrified and driven by instinctual fear, Damian stood up and ran back home to his parents. He ran and ran, yet it felt as if he were running in place, trapped in some twisted dream, like Zeno's paradox, where the distance between him and his destination seemed both near and infinitely far at the same time. It was as if time itself were bending and stretching beneath his feet. A murder of crows perched in a nearby tree, watching him, their sinister calls echoing in mockery. When Damian finally reached the entrance of his building, he looked back and saw the black fire creeping closer, just a hundred meters away. At that moment, his fear transformed into desperation and resolve. He thought of his parents. He called upon Braisis for aid and armed only with his will to protect those he loved and his faithful companion, he faced what now seemed like his inevitable doom. With no second thought, he dove into the black fire in a final attempt to rip it apart. He did not know exactly what he was doing, he acted purely on instinct. Even now, he does not fully remember what happened next, or whether he did anything at all. But he recalls tearing through the black fire and everything within it, only to find three female figures standing side by side.

He stepped back in shock.

The three women moved forward, equidistant from one another, their bodies almost touching, gliding toward him with a peaceful, graceful air. Their movements were perfectly synchronized, mirroring one another as though they were bound by a single will. Each was dressed in a flowing, crocheted chiton, with closed, flat shoes resembling modern-day Ferragamo, a full body underlayer that covered the skin beneath the chiton, and delicately sewn gloves. Their presence was striking, yet each had a distinct appearance. The figure on the left was completely white, an ultra-pure, glowing white. The one in the middle was royal purple, her entire form bathed in that deep, regal hue. The figure on the right had a white base adorned with nine horizontal bands of brownish orange. The bands were most vibrant at the top, gradually fading into the white before another band interrupted the transition, creating a rhythmic pattern of color.

Damian, captivated, tried to peer beyond the veil of the figure in the center. The moment he did, a flood of visions overwhelmed him.

The visions played like a film in his mind. A panoramic view of a pristine, untouched landscape dominated his field of vision. Time accelerated, unfolding in a non-verbal, visual narrative. The sounds of nature filled his ears, the rumbling of the earth, the rushing of rivers, the whistling of the wind, the crackling of fire deep within volcanoes. He watched as vegetation of all kinds flourished. At the heart of it all, a magnificent oak tree took root and grew, its branches stretching wide. From beneath its canopy, a female figure emerged, her body sprouting from the roots, her head adorned with small, ram-like horns. The female figure grew, and the three other women were seen playing with her, as if they were her mothers. Soon after, two additional figures entered the field, a man and a woman. These two, however, remained near a towering sequoia-like tree that bore golden-hued fruit. The male and female figures, who appeared humanoid or human-like, eventually procreated and spread rapidly across the landscape, multiplying like wildfire.

As time passed, the world transitioned from a vibrant, Spring-like era of birth and renewal into a heated, Summer-like age, a time of peak vitality, abundance, and indulgence. Damian was reminded of the left and center panels of Bosch's *The Garden of Earthly Delights*, where life was at its most lush and exuberant. Eventually, some descendants of these original human-like beings intermingled with the horned female figure and her kin, creating a hybrid lineage. However, conflict soon arose. In what appeared to be a territorial struggle, the human-like peoples turned against those who had interbred with the horned female's lineage. Through deception, they lured them into a distant, isolated field and, in an act of betrayal, slaughtered the horned female figure along with her progeny.

In response, the three female figures were seen wailing in grief and rage, cursing the very elements, earth, wind, water, and fire, upon which humanity depended. The human-like people, despite their treachery, continued to evolve, procreate, and expand their dominion over the environment. This marked the onset of a more somber, Fall-like era, a time of slow decline and impending decay. Signs of humanity's rapid evolution became evident. Yet, with each step forward, the three female figures remained ever-present, bringing calamity, war, famine, pestilence, and mass death. However, these destructive forces were intermittently counterbalanced by external interventions that sought to shield humanity from total annihilation.

This cycle persisted until the dawn of the Industrial Revolution. At this point, a much darker, Winter-like night settled upon the landscape, casting a shadow over all that had once flourished. Under the pale glow of a waning crescent moon, nocturnal creatures, emerged serpents slithered, owls perched in silent watch, crows cawed ominously, and the howls of wild dogs and hyenas echoed through the night. Then, from the marshy ground in front of the ancient oak tree, a monstrous figure arose, a golem, forged from decayed trees and the remnants of dead animals. Its limbs were twisted branches, yet its core pulsed with the internal organs of beasts.

The three female figures gathered around the grotesque being. With deliberate precision, they infused it with life, animating the lifeless mass using animal blood as a conduit for their dark magic. The vision accelerated. The landscape's devastation unfolded at an ever-increasing pace. The human-like beings had changed, they had grown distant from nature, obsessed with technological augmentation and tools. At every turn, nature was sacrificed in pursuit of progress, until their very essence was transferred into inorganic vessels, severing their last ties to the living world.

At last, the final stage of devastation was reached.

Then, the vision shifted. The three female figures now stood at the center of the ruined expanse, the only source of light in a world swallowed by darkness. Even the moon's reflection had vanished, leaving only their spectral glow.

They turned to Damian and, in unison, asked:

"What will you do, Damian, our White Snake?"

Death

It had long weighed on the child's consciousness that the illness and malaise of his early years had transformed his parents' faces. His close brushes with death, both physical and metaphysical, had often reinvigorated his desire to live. Yet constraint, pain, and guilt remained constant companions. He looked from the window of the old, dilapidated hospital and saw some children playing in the streets. Kairon anguished, longing to join them and travel to the countryside, his favorite pastimes. He remembered wandering through the hills and valleys, meeting country folk, and pretending to "hunt" birds. The laughter of the children outside the hospital and that of his friends in his memories merged, creating an exalted feeling of hope and a yearning to live. But to live without conditions, without restraints, and worst of all, without the painful uncertainty of an unknown future.

He had a decision to make, or so he thought, for he was just a child. What everyone knew, however, was that the latest sudden, chaotic episode of ill health had left an indelible mark on the lives of those around him. For Kairon, it had been painful and brief, yet full of fear and desperation. For others, it was heavier and darker. One night, Kairon woke at 10:03 a.m. to awaken his parents, feeling the strange sensation that often preceded such bouts of illness.

"Mama, Mama, I'm not feeling well."

"What's wrong, my child?"

"I feel funny again. My throat itches, and I'm thirsty."

What seemed like an innocent conversation carried alarming undertones of crisis based on experience.

"Come here, child, sit next to me. It's nothing, don't worry," the mother lied in a desperate attempt to comfort him and wish away another episode of helplessness and despair.

"Try to go to sleep. It's nothing; you may have had a nightmare you don't remember."

Kairon tried to go back to sleep. Meanwhile, his mother asked his father to get water quietly, hoping Kairon would sleep. At this point, Kairon either fell asleep or entered a delirium; he still does not know. It was then that he had his first encounter with death.

"Mama, who is that man standing in the corner?" the child asked in a raspy voice.

"Who are you talking about, my child?"

"There, the man holding some water in his hands. He's strange. Why is he hiding his face and body under those black hooded robes? Something is wrong with him."

Kairon did not hear an answer from his mother. Whether she had answered or not, he did not know. Instead, he heard the eerie shriek of the man in the corner, akin to the sound of unfathomable pain and grief. The man's form constantly shifted. He moved like dark shadows through the room, transmuting from a full pale body to an emaciated one, to a form marked by decay, to a skeleton, and finally to darkness cloaked under robes. This transformation repeated. Kairon was thirsty, but something warned him not to accept the water, which he rejected from the hands of the mysterious man now standing at the edge of his bed. This rejection seemed to anger the figure. At this point, Kairon began feeling worse, and his vision started to fail. He hadn't realized it, but he had stopped breathing. His lungs had been deprived of air for what seemed an eternity to his parents. Kairon tried communicating with them, but no air came to his lungs. Every desperate attempt to signal his fear and pain only worsened the situation. Without realizing it, he had started pulling at his mother's hair and gesticulating wildly while gasping for air. Soon, his vision failed entirely, and everything went dark.

A while later, Kairon awoke in the back seat of a car, on his way to the hospital with his parents and a neighbor who owned the car. He passed out again from exhaustion, fear, and pain. Meanwhile, questions plagued his parents' minds, bubbling up from a place of fear, guilt, desperation, and anger. What had their child done to deserve this? What had they done to deserve this? Why was this happening? Why him and not them? Most importantly, they asked themselves: What could they do to resolve this? What was the best course of action? These last two questions paralyzed them.

This experience profoundly changed Kairon. He couldn't stop thinking about the mysterious man in the room and his desire to rid himself of this debilitating condition. From his hospital bed, he overheard his parents speaking with doctors about the solution: a risky operation or an equally uncertain and precarious alternative. That's when Kairon saw it again, a dark shadow bouncing around the room out of the corner of his eye. He felt a presence watching, waiting. Yet he was not afraid; he was resolute. In desperation, he silently called for intervention, no matter the source. He just wanted relief. Nothing answered. Kairon heard faint whistling, found it strange, but dismissed it" He 'ell asleep, weak and convalescing from the demanding ordeal.

A few days later, Kairon returned home from the hospital to much anticipation from the neighborhood and his family. Though he tried to forget the experience and sought to reunite with his friends as if nothing had happened, the memory lingered. He disliked talking about it. When asked, he would brush it off, joking, "Episode? It all feels like a half-forgotten nightmare now lost to oblivion." After all, he was just a child who wanted to play and enjoy life without fully understanding the weight of his experiences.

One day, while playing with his friends, Kairon saw the father of one of his friends, Carlos, speaking with his parents. Carlos was known in the neighborhood as a difficult, reserved man with a reputation for practicing witchcraft. Kairon recalled overhearing his parents' dismissive remarks about Carlos offering to help him during an earlier health crisis. "What we need is a doctor, not a witch doctor," his father had said. When Kairon asked about the man, his parents warned him to stay away from Carlos and his house. He didn't question their advice and rarely thought about it again until he saw Carlos talking to his parents. Later, Carlos's son, Richard, invited Kairon and the neighborhood kids to play soccer near their home. Knowing his parents' disapproval of Carlos, Kairon avoided mentioning where they were going. Instead, he simply told them he was playing soccer with his friends. Overjoyed to see him healthy and happy again, his parents didn't press for details.

The group gathered outside Richard's home, near a vacant lot that had been converted into a goat and pig pen. Carlos's livestock were well-regarded, and the pens became a backdrop for their soccer games. Kairon and his friends played energetically, enjoying the warm day. At one point, the game moved to the lower entrance of a nearby building. The entrance, though a common play spot, was known for its damaged electrical outlet with exposed wires. Though it hadn't been functional for years, no one paid it much mind.

While playing, Kairon positioned himself near the outlet. During an intense play, he stumbled, and his foot tangled in the exposed wires. To everyone's shock, a sudden burst of electricity surged through the cables. Kairon collapsed. When Kairon came to, strange sounds filled his ears, the clanking of chains, echoing voices, and the hammering of metal. The noise reminded him of his friend Rafael's father's blacksmith shop. But these sounds soon gave way to guttural cries of agony and torment that paralyzed him with fear. Though he dared not move, Kairon felt the presence of shadowy figures passing by. He shut his eyes tightly, willing himself to wake up. The noises eventually subsided. "It's over," he thought, trying to convince himself it had been another nightmare.

But when he opened his eyes, Kairon saw spectral forms pacing in confusion and sorrow. Some seemed tormented; others moved aimlessly, unaware of their surroundings. As Kairon watched in horror, a few of the specters noticed him and began moving toward him. Panicked, he tried to escape, but the shadows surrounded him. He woke abruptly to find himself lying on the building floor, surrounded by his friends. Their relieved laughter greeted him.

"Bro, the weirdest stuff always happens to you," one joked.

"Yeah, you're like a magnet for strange things," added another. "How did you even get shocked by those old wires?"

Though Kairon laughed along, the incident unsettled him deeply. Reflecting on his friends' teasing, he couldn't deny the strange frequency of his experiences. Yet, like before, he pushed the memory aside and rejoined the game.

The day's events took another turn when Kairon fell onto some rusty metal pipes, cutting his arm badly. The wound bled profusely, alarming Richard, who ran to fetch his father. Carlos arrived quickly, assessing the injury. "Enough play for today," he announced, sending the other children home. Turning to Kairon, he said, "Come inside. Let me help you with that cut." Despite his parents' warnings, Kairon hesitated. He felt both a sense of duty to accept Carlos's help and a deep curiosity about the man and his rumored powers. Finally, he followed Carlos into the house, unsure of what awaited him.

All the other kids laughed and joked, but deep down, Kairon reflected on their comments and found a painful truth in them. He pushed those thoughts aside, though, as the group decided to play soccer near the animal pens. Kairon and his friends played for another hour, and everything seemed to have settled. But not long after, Kairon fell onto some old iron pipes, slicing his arm deeply. Blood poured from the wound, and Richard, panicked by the sight, ran to get his father.

When Richard's father, Carlos, arrived, he saw Kairon's bleeding arm and immediately told the children to go home, declaring playtime over. Turning to Kairon, he said, "Come with me. Let's take care of that cut." Kairon hesitated, his parents' warnings ringing in his ears. He tried to decline. "I'll just go home. It's fine," he muttered.

"Nonsense," Carlos said firmly. "Come inside."

Conflicted, Kairon felt both a sense of obligation to accept Carlos's help and an inexplicable pull toward the house, as though something unseen was urging him forward. He finally relented and stepped inside. Years later, Kairon recounted the events in a letter to his friend Gustavo:

> *".....I went to Carlos's house to get help with my cut but, as I now see clearly, also for my condition. The house was*

clean and peaceful. Carlos told me to come in, and I did. He was very kind, taking care of the cut first. The bleeding stopped almost immediately, and I still have the scar to this day, proof of the incident. But then Carlos told me something unexpected. He said I needed spiritual help. He claimed to have consulted with his spirits of the dead, who revealed that I needed protection from the powers of Death itself. Death, he said, was willing to protect me, but only if I became its servant. He explained that the spirits wanted me to work with them as their supreme necromancer.

Carlos pointed to a witch cauldron hidden behind some netting and beads. He told me he would pass it to me, that it would help me fulfill this role. The cauldron was made of black cast iron, covered in what looked like decayed matter, with sticks and other metal objects adorning it. The top half of a skull was faintly visible. I thanked him for his offer but told him I wasn't sure this was right for me. Carlos insisted, but I politely declined and left in a hurry.

That night, I dreamed about the same thing. In the dream, I was back in his house. Carlos was once again offering me the witch cauldron. This time, I accepted it. It was smaller in the dream, made of gray metal and fitting neatly in my hands. Carlos then led me to a part of the yard I hadn't seen before, behind the animal pens. He asked me to stand in the center of the space, holding the cauldron, while he sang incantations in a language that sounded very ancient but unrecognizable. He drew sigils and diagrams on the ground around me.

Then, Carlos took a branch and made a shallow cut along my Achilles tendon, moving upward. It didn't hurt much. He continued singing, shaking the branch, and striking the ground and my body with it. As he did, the cauldron seemed to grow heavier. A second head, resembling a large porcelain doll, appeared inside it. The vibrations and pulsating power from the cauldron were overwhelming. After some time, I can't say how long, since it was a dream, a figurine inside the cauldron straightened and stood upright. Carlos then took the cauldron from me and walked away. When I looked at his face, his eyes were white, like a blind man's, and he wore a malevolent smile.

He began speaking in a strange, distorted voice, as though to someone I couldn't see.

He said, 'You, servant of the cauldron, you're acting like a fool. Why don't you tell him the truth? Tell him that he is wanted by the power of lightning, destructive fire, and the god of Olympus himself. The dark, shadow side of Jupiter does not want him to suffer the disturbances and hunger of death again.' Carlos tried to hand me the cauldron, now engulfed in flames. But another voice, higher-pitched and distorted, spoke. It rejected me, saying I was ugly and unworthy.

Carlos argued with the voice, speaking in the same ventriloquist-like tone. After some back-and-forth, the voice relented, agreeing that the spirit of the cauldron should serve me. At that moment, I noticed a black, jewel-encrusted rickshaw in the corner of my eye. Carlos gestured for me to sit in it, promising that if I accepted, my life would be as easy as a ride in the rickshaw. But his eyes betrayed a dark ulterior motive, and I felt repelled.

I rejected the offer. Even in my sleep, I knew better than to accept. But that wasn't the end of the dream. The scene shifted to a dimly lit room filled with taxidermized animals, old wooden furniture, and fur and leather garments hanging from racks. A hooded figure screeched and flew across the room, its movements erratic and terrifying. Oddly, I wasn't afraid. Instead, I felt an intense desire to confront it. I chased the figure as it tried to hide inside the furniture and clothes. Eventually, I cornered it at a rack of garments. When it leaped at me in a final attempt to escape, I felt it fuse with me. In that moment, I saw my reflection intertwined with the figure's, our images inseparable.

Then I woke up.

After that night, I stayed away from Carlos and Richard's house for good. I never saw them again. Strangely, my condition improved. I've never suffered from it since. What do you think, Gustavo? Was it just a child's vivid imagination? Or was it something more? All I can say is that the dream remains as vivid today as it was then. Make of it what you will...."

Epitaph

In silence mastered, in discipline forged.
In delay patience, in wounds embalmed.
In boundaries and isolation mysteries.
What is gained and who is lost?

In pain truth, in responsibility meaning.
In aging grace, in reflection wisdom.
In challenges and obstacles maturity.
What is gained and who is lost?

In existence endurance, in trials strength.
In death melancholy, in awareness peace.
In time and contemplation seriousness.
What is gained and who is lost?

Oracles

On the eve of Holy Week, *Annus Dei* 2017, Ernesto had developed some strange ideas about contacting the dead and touching the fabric of the universe itself. Perhaps it was because he was tired of the mundane, tired of the unrest, the monotony, and the limitations of what he perceived as his lot in life, or maybe it was simply because he felt intellectually bored and unchallenged. Not that he had any real reason for such feelings, nor that he was born into a poor or oppressed family, but rather because he had been born into a middle-class one, and he felt he had peaked early or so he thought.

He had a stable job, a fiancée, and friends whom he loved, but he often deemed and even exclaimed out loud, that this could not be enough.

And so, Ernesto had begun exploring the occult and the esoteric during his downtime, and even during working hours, at his job at the museum. The museum was, in fact, a late 19th- to early 20th-century French pharmacy and drugstore that had been converted into a museum due to its historical significance as a scientific institution. It was also quite large, with a first floor consisting of the public-facing portion, a large landing area, and a wide marble stairwell with intricately ornamented iron railings leading to an equally expansive second floor.

The second floor primarily consisted of the living quarters, a small kitchen, numerous paintings, a personal library, and a grand piano situated on the landing. To the right of the stairwell was a long corridor that led to the backroom of the public-facing portion of the pharmacy. The floor was laid in checkered gray and black marble. Here, the wood furniture was made of European white beech, and this was the most densely packed area. One could find a vast collection of scientific instruments, including weights, percolators, lixiviators, alembics, mortars, measuring cups, Championer vaporizers, presses (including one shaped like a crocodile and made of bronze), scarifiers, electrocardiographic machines, and other gynecologic and obstetric instruments used for midwifery and emergencies. There were also very large prescription books and formulae, as well as early chemical structures of important compounds and their reactions.

To the right and toward the back of this area, and the public-facing section, was a large open space featuring a combination of mahogany counters and display cabinets, as well as European white beech furniture and shelving. These shelves held medicines in a variety of containers, some porcelain, some glass, either displayed behind glass or left open. There were numerous beakers, mortars, and other chemistry tools, such as graduated cylinders and distillation kits, including Bunsen burners. This area was built in a fully open-layout architectural style, square in size, with a balcony-like loft on the second floor. To the back of these areas was the large open-concept kitchen, with a spacious yet atrium-like courtyard that featured hanging ferns suspended from iron hangers affixed to the walls of the second floor. The kitchen included large iron versions of the chemical tools found in the previous room, which were used to cook and distill industrial-sized chemical reactions in the back kitchen. This was done to produce the medicines sold at the pharmacy.

The kitchen was centered around a very large coal oven, with a broader, square section to the left that was used for distillation. It also featured four smaller compartments, each with door openings of varying sizes. The oven was lined with white tiles, which also covered the wall panels behind the oven to form a clean and uniform backdrop.

Yet, the front-facing section was the more elaborate and intricate. It consisted of intricately carved mahogany counters, façades, and shelves; marble countertops; a manual counterweight scale; and a very large assortment of medically accepted prescriptions and therapies, as well as experimental ones from that era. These medications and treatments now adorned the museum as its most valuable items. Some were encased in highly elaborate porcelain *soupières* and vases of various colors; others were stored inside transparent and ornate glass vessels that typically contained liquids or items of distinct and striking coloration. Still others were placed in enclosed rotating glass displays and shelves for secure viewing.

Among these was one of the museum's most medically significant jars: it contained scorpions and their venom, which had been experimented on earlier in the 20th century as a possible cure for cancer.

In the center of the room, there were three open doors. Inside the arch of the main one stood a large marble statue of the Virgin Mary, typically adorned with flowers and other Marian iconography. Another striking and memorable detail of the museum was its painted glass. This was Ernesto's favorite feature. Late in the afternoon, he would often stand in this part of the museum and contemplate the way light filtered through the painted glass. He would muse on its beauty and daydream about the great cathedrals of Europe, with their ornate stained-glass windows, imagining himself visiting them one day. These moments served as a form of solace during heavy work periods.

In fact, these instances of self-reflection and quasi-mystical experience were what had led to his disillusionment with his job and the monotony of what he considered his mundane existence.

Hence, the museum, once a dream come true and a fulfilling, challenging career, had now turned boring and predictable in Ernesto's eyes. He would often find excuses to leave during lunchtime to meet with his best friends, Daniel and Dagoberto, in the park square outside the museum.

And so, with near clockwork predictability, Ernesto escaped to the park for lunch to meet his friends. Usually, he was the first to arrive and the last to leave, but this time, his friends were already there. They were playing chess on one of the concrete benches that had been converted into a makeshift chessboard by interlaying checkered black and white tiles. Daniel was beating Dagoberto, as usual, and Ernesto was content not to play against Dagoberto this time. He had managed to beat Dagoberto on a few occasions, something Daniel had never done, but those wins were rare.

Daniel worked as a dentist in the corner office on the lower left-hand crossroad leading to the square, while Dagoberto worked as a librarian on the opposite corner of the same intersection. The friends greeted each other with enthusiasm and roasted one another a bit, as was customary between them.

Ernesto pulled out his packed lunch: a swordfish sandwich with some lettuce, lemon, and pepper, along with a soursop fruit and a bottle of water. He ate quietly while his friends continued their game, and Dagoberto entered the endgame of their second match. After finishing his meal, Ernesto lit one of his favorite Black Perique box American Spirit cigarettes and began to talk about his recent lackluster attitude at work.

To his surprise, Daniel and Dagoberto shared the same sentiment. This quickly led them to reminiscing, liberally romanticizing, their youth and old shenanigans. They revisited the usual topics: girlfriends, parties, recreational drug use, and the occasional terrifying car accidents during races or fights.

At one point, Daniel brought up, somewhat mournfully, his torn meniscus and broken arms, the injuries that forced him to retire early from track and field. Both Ernesto and Dagoberto expressed regret, as Daniel had been quite good and was on track to join the national team within two seasons.

This, in turn, reminded them of the time they fought against a rival gang of boys from the next city over. During the confrontation, one of the rival boys pulled an AK from the trunk of his car and aimed it at Dagoberto. As always, Dagoberto thanked Ernesto for stepping up in that moment, for saying that if the guy was going to do something, he'd have to deal with both. Even Ernesto didn't know why he had done that.

Luckily, someone from the rival crew pretended to be friendly with Ernesto, which helped de-escalate the situation. Ernesto brushed it off at the time, but now, as an adult, he often pondered the moment, scolding himself for his childhood bravado and inflated confidence. He was just glad nothing had happened.

However, even this trip down memory lane wasn't enough to shake their shared discontent. They all recognized the boredom saturating their lives and began discussing plans for the weekend. At first, they talked about going to the nearby resort town to party, but even that felt tired, and, besides, their partners probably wouldn't be thrilled about it.

Especially Richie, Daniel's partner, who was notoriously jealous. Daniel had been quite the ladies' man in his youth and remained fit and active, even now. Dagoberto, for his part, was married to Julia, his high school sweetheart, and they had three young children, so he was almost guaranteed not to get away for an extended weekend.

Ernesto, on the other hand, was used to Sonia's long hours at the national laboratory. He knew she would be working overtime this weekend, trying to catch up on a phase-two clinical trial her team had been pressured to advance.

And so, it was at this moment that Daniel brought it up, the topic they had all sworn never to speak of again in their adulthood, out of shame and fear:

"What about the time we went to the cemetery to play with Johana's Ouija board, guys?" Daniel asked, raising an eyebrow, half-expecting them to change the subject.

However, to his surprise, both Ernesto and Dagoberto now wanted to talk about it.

"Yesss. I remember that day... quite scary," said Dagoberto, with a strange intonation and an odd deflection in his voice.

"I don't know, guys... that was some heavy shit. I'm still not sure what happened that day," said Ernesto.

"I don't know," both Dagoberto and Daniel echoed, though dissonantly.

"You know she's now a full-on medium and witch, right?" said Dagoberto.

"Who, Johana?" asked Ernesto.

"Yeah. She came to a conference on Magick, Mysticism, and Witchcraft that we held at the library last month. I saw her there.

71

She's renowned for her powers and seems to be quite respected. She gave a presentation on scrying," Dagoberto said.

"Didn't you go out with her, Ernesto?" asked Daniel.

"Yeah, I did, but only for a summer," Ernesto replied.

They teased him for it, as Johana had always been a bit strange, and now she was a full-blown witch. The conversation derailed for a moment into playful mockery. Ernesto went along with it, he had a good relationship with them, after all. And besides, he knew it was true: he had always liked the weird and wild girls.

After a while, though, the laughter faded. A few minutes of silence followed as each of them glanced at their watches. Ernesto noticed this and, not wanting to return to work just yet decided to break the lull.

"Come on, guys, be honest. We're adults now. One of you was pulling our leg, right?" Ernesto asked.

"What do you mean?" said Dagoberto.

"Yeah, what are you talking about, Ernesto?" Daniel added.

"Are you guys really going to keep up the farce? Come on, there's no way that planchette moved by itself," said Ernesto.

"Then how do you explain the fact that when we asked the spirit to make itself present, *you*, Daniel, who was lying down on one of the benches listening to music, music we could both hear, suddenly stood up and said you felt something sit on your lap?" asked Dagoberto.

"What about the shadows you said you saw, Ernesto?" he continued.

"And the fact that the spirit told us it was Jewish, and we were in a Jewish cemetery, which we hadn't even noticed until then?" added Daniel. "Most, if not all, of the headstones had the Star of David on them."

"Yeah," said both Ernesto and Dagoberto, one after the other, echoing each other's answer a few times.

Another silence fell over the conversation, but this time it carried a denser, more distinct weight. It was as if the atmosphere itself had shifted, like the drop in millibar pressure before a winter storm.

"What if we did it again, Ernesto? Would you dare? Come on, you're a man of science, what are you afraid of?" said Daniel, half-joking, goading Ernesto with a smirk.

"I don't care. Let's do it. But only if Dagoberto comes. I want Dagoberto there in case you try one of your mischievous tricks," said Ernesto.

"Don't know what you're talking about. Hahaha," Daniel replied.

"Hahaha. Daniel scarred you for life with his senior year pranks!" added Dagoberto, laughing.

"Hahahaa. Well, you are too! Or have you forgotten when…"

"Well, well. Water under the bridge," Dagoberto interjected quickly, grinning.

"Hahaha!" Ernesto belly laughed.

"But where are we going to get a Ouija board? Last time we borrowed Johana's, but I don't know who has one now," said Ernesto.

"That I can solve," said Dagoberto.

"Last month, during the conference where Johana and a group of other practitioners, including *paleros*, *santeros*, ceremonial magicians, scryers, tarotists, astrologers, spiritists, and *babalawos*, who presented their divination tools, they brought in various examples for demonstration. According to them, especially the *paleros*, this time of year, when Christ descends into the underworld, is when the most malevolent practitioners take the opportunity to do dark works and malefic magick. The *paleros* say they turn the crucifix upside down in their *ngangas* and perform the most harmful rituals. They also said this is when the underworld and otherworldly forces are most active and present in our world."

"You know, it's interesting, during Johana's presentation, she spoke about Saturn and its association with the devil. She pointed out a curious idea: even though Saturn is often linked with dark forces and black magick, especially those opposing life, it's actually Saturn's iconography that most closely resembles Jesus's. First, because Jesus is said to have been born under the constellation of

Saturn, and second due to the old Saturnalia festival, where social roles were inverted, the poor made rich, and the rich made poor.

"But even more intriguing is the symbolism. Saturn represents the cross of matter over spirit, similar to the Christian cross, representing the dominance of the material over the spiritual. In contrast, and contrary to popular belief, it's Jupiter's symbol that represents spirit over the cross of matter, and that symbol, when inverted, is the one *paleros* associate with dark and malefic occult practices. Johana also mentioned something about the Golden Age of Saturn, but I didn't quite get that. Hahaha…

"You know what? Getting back to the topic, some of the practitioners left their tools with us at our request for the museum's collection. Among them was a Ouija board brought by Johana. We could borrow it and use it."

"Problem solved," said Ernesto.

"But where are we going to use it? We're a bit old to be jumping fences to get into cemeteries," said Daniel.

"How about we use it in the museum?" suggested Ernesto.

"The museum?" both Daniel and Dagoberto said in surprised unison.

"Yeah. According to the staff, the museum is *quite* haunted," Ernesto said with an air of intentional mystery. "The night shift workers and security guards have all shared their experiences, hearing footsteps on the second floor, cabinets and closet doors opening and closing by themselves, and things moving or falling to the floor."

"Yeah, but that happens in old buildings. It could be considered what Jung called a catalytic experience. Nothing more," responded Daniel.

"What about the times the staff have heard the grand piano play by itself? Or the cleaning staff who've been pushed, and had their hair pulled, while working on the second floor?" smirked Ernesto.

"What? No, no, no. Come on, guys. I'm too old for this," said Dagoberto.

"Hahahah!"

"Hahahah," Daniel and Ernesto laughed in unison.

"You afraid, Dagoberto?" teased Ernesto.

"I'm not. I'm just worried about bringing something home to my kids, that's all," replied Dagoberto.

Both Daniel and Ernesto gave him an ironic look, clearly not buying the excuse.

"Okay, then. Let's do it. But don't come crying to me later if weird shit starts happening in your life, just saying," added Dagoberto.

"Alright then, it's settled. We'll use the Ouija, and we'll use it in Ernesto's museum," said Daniel.

"That works for me," said Ernesto, to which Dagoberto nodded in agreement, his head moving up and down.

"This is what we'll do," Ernesto continued. "I'll light the kerosene lamp at the front entrance when I'm ready to let everyone in. So keep an eye out for the museum chemist's lantern. It's to the right of the right-hand door of the building. Remember, there are four large doors, don't use the others. They tend to screech very loudly. Sounds almost haunted. Hahahah," he added playfully.

Soon after, the friends said their goodbyes, they had taken longer than expected to return to work from lunch. But Ernesto stayed behind for a moment. He didn't feel like going back just yet and wanted to take in the air a bit longer.

"Besides," he thought to himself,

I'm the manager, and today is Saturday the 8th*. No one's interested in visiting a pharmaceutical museum at this day and time. Olga, the senior museum guide, can take care of any visitors, if any group even shows up.*

~

When Ernesto lit the lantern at 3:00 AM, a deep fog had settled over the colonial square where the museum was located. The lantern was barely visible from afar but still bright enough to catch the eyes of Daniel and Dagoberto, who had been waiting on one of the wooden benches in Liberty Park, near the central statue.

Dagoberto noticed it first and quietly alerted Daniel by bumping his arm with an elbow. Daniel jumped but, seeing Dagoberto pointing, immediately understood what he was indicating. They got up right away and walked over to the museum entrance.

But the door was closed.

Ernesto had shut it out of force of habit.

They knocked hesitantly a few times before Ernesto finally came to open it. When he did, they had a brief but tense exchange, each expressing frustration with the other for not following through on the plan, until Ernesto realized it had been his oversight. He apologized to both Daniel and Dagoberto.

As they stepped inside, footsteps were heard above them, on the second floor.

Daniel immediately whispered, "Is there someone else here?" His tone was surprised, edged with fear at the possibility of being caught inside the museum at this hour.

"No, no. There's no one here at this hour," Ernesto replied.

"This is what you were talking about, wasn't it?" said Dagoberto.

Ernesto nodded and gestured for them to head up to the second floor, where, according to him, the most activity took place.

When they reached the landing, they saw the grand piano Ernesto had mentioned. It looked old and poorly maintained. There was nothing particularly special about it, most of the museum's preservation budget went to the first floor and the medical inventory. The second floor, originally the living quarters, had been converted into research offices and archives, though some paintings and personal items were still kept there.

Ernesto suggested they use one of the offices, since it had chairs and a large bureau.

Dagoberto, who had brought the Ouija board in his backpack, pulled it out and handed it to Ernesto.

"Here you go. Take it. By the way, is this the same one we borrowed from Johana back in high school?"

"Let me see… Hmm. I'm not sure. It looks familiar, but to me, all these things look the same," said Ernesto.

"Same," added Daniel.

"Well, never mind that, let's just use it. It's already 3:25," blurted Ernesto, sounding almost rushed, as if eager to get it over with... or as if something deep inside him was afraid.

The friends placed the board in the center of the room, lit a small office lamp, and turned off the main ceiling light. Naively, they believed that the dim ambience would create a better atmosphere for ghosts to manifest.

They began by asking a few questions, all three of them holding the planchette. At first, the planchette didn't move, but they did hear footsteps and the sound of a door opening. Daniel stood up and went to check it out, but returned shrugging, gesturing that he had no idea what it was.

They continued, but the planchette remained still. After about fifteen minutes of trying, Dagoberto sighed and said he was tired, that nothing was happening. He added that this had been a childish idea from the start and that they needed to grow up and stop clinging to their younger days.

"For God's sake, we're three mature professionals, playing with a Ouija board on a Sunday morning."

Right as he said this, the planchette jerked suddenly, then began to move continuously, straight toward the "Yes" on the board.

Without hesitation, Ernesto and Dagoberto turned to Daniel, certain he was playing one of his old practical jokes.

"Come on, Daniel. Really?" said Dagoberto.

"Hey, for real, man, come on!" added Ernesto.

"What are you guys talking about? I haven't moved the planchette. *You* are!" Daniel retorted.

Daniel lifted his hands from the planchette, and it stopped moving immediately.

The other two immediately blamed him.

Daniel grew mildly infuriated with them for accusing him. He insisted that he hadn't pushed it, that he was actually curious about it moving. He pleaded with them to try again, just the two of them, to see if the board would respond without him.

Ernesto and Dagoberto conceded, mostly out of fatigue. They just wanted to go home, and figured if they humored Daniel, it would be over quickly. They still believed he'd been the one moving it.

The two placed their hands on the planchette again and asked:

"Are there any spirits present here with us?"

At first, the planchette didn't move. Then, all of a sudden, it glided toward the "Yes" section of the board, until the glass window at its center rested directly over the word.

"Aha! What did I say? I didn't move it!" said Daniel. "Did one of *you* move it?"

Neither Dagoberto nor Ernesto said anything.

Then Dagoberto turned to Ernesto and accused him of pushing the planchette, only for Ernesto to vehemently deny it.

Daniel told Dagoberto to calm down, reminding him that not everyone was out to get him. He added that he believed Ernesto.

Dagoberto, clearly unsettled now, said:

"Let me try it by myself. I want to see if it moves when I'm alone."

"I've heard it doesn't work like that, that you need at least two people," said Daniel.

"You guys are just trying to trick me," responded Dagoberto.

"Let him," said Ernesto.

Dagoberto asked if the spirit was near them. The planchette didn't move.

"You, see? You bastards, playing tricks on me," said Dagoberto, pulling his hands away.

"Let me try by myself, Dagoberto," said Ernesto.

"And what would *that* prove?" exclaimed Dagoberto.

"I just want to try," Ernesto replied calmly.

He placed his hands on top of the planchette, much to Dagoberto's displeasure, and asked: "Are there any spirits present in the pharmacy who would like to communicate with us?"

To everyone's surprise, most of all Ernesto's, the planchette moved toward "Yes" and hovered over it. All three of them were stunned.

Then Daniel said he wanted to try it by himself. But when he placed his hands on the planchette, it didn't move.

At that point, Dagoberto insisted it had to be Ernesto. "It's you. It's been you all along. You're playing tricks on us."

But Ernesto, dumbfounded by what had just happened, the way the planchette had moved with force under his hands, proposed a solution.

"If you think I'm lying, if you think I'm messing with you, let's put it to the test. Tell me to ask something that only *you* know the answer to."

"Hmmm... Hmmm... Don't play with that," responded Dagoberto.

"Don't play with *what*, Dagoberto? Come on, give me something to ask. Something only you would know."

Dagoberto hesitated for a long moment. But with Daniel's insistence, he finally said:

"Ask it about my sister. Where is she?"

Both Ernesto and Daniel were stunned.

They had never heard Dagoberto mention having a sister, *ever*.

Still, Ernesto assumed it was a ruse, some kind of setup to test him. So he asked the question, using Dagoberto's full name:

"Where is Dagoberto's sister?"

The planchette began to move.

It spelled out: *T-H-E O-C-E-A-N*

Dagoberto went pale.

Both Ernesto and Daniel noticed.

"Dagoberto, what happened? What is it?" Daniel asked.

Dagoberto turned to Ernesto, eyes wide.

"How? Just how? How did you do that?"

"Do what?" Ernesto was visibly confused. "Could you tell us what's going on? Why have you turned pale?"

Dagoberto, collecting himself from a brief sobbing spell, shared that when he was a child, his parents had lost his infant sister to an unknown illness, later diagnosed as Sudden Infant Death Syndrome. His parents had eventually scattered her ashes in the ocean, since she had been born on the feast day of the *Virgen de las Mercedes.*

Daniel was stunned, but even more so was Ernesto.

Trying to lighten the mood, Ernesto then asked the board a more playful question: "Will I marry Sonia?"

He expected a straightforward yes, something to bring them back to normalcy.

But the planchette quickly slid to No.

This surprised him. He laughed it off out loud, making fun of the response, until a loud bang sounded from the first floor.

They all stopped talking and stared at one another.

"Should we check if someone got in?" asked Daniel, half-standing.

"Wait... let's ask it something else. What do you want to ask, Daniel?" said Ernesto, trying to stay calm.

"Ask if it's the spirit of Dr. Triolet, the main pharmacist," said Daniel.

Ernesto found that a good question and posed it to the board.

The planchette moved decisively to No.

Just then, the piano outside the office began to play.

It sounded like the work of Camille Saint-Saëns.

The friends fell silent, listening. The music couldn't have played for more than a minute, but when they were about to ask who was playing, the piano stopped. Daniel was about to suggest asking anyway when they were interrupted by a loud, unmistakable voice with a heavy Spanish accent:

"*¡Trabaja, negro! ¡Tira el carbón en el horno, que no se prende ni se mantiene solo, coño!!*"

This was followed by the crack of a whip.

Another voice cried out in pain:

"*Aaaahhhh... ¡Ayyyyy! ¡No po' avor', o' suplico!*"

The cries were accompanied by the grinding sound of iron shackles and chains rubbing against bone. The friends were deeply disturbed, not just by the sounds themselves, but by their unmistakable colonial undertones. The language, the cruelty, it all felt out of place, yet it forced them to confront the unspoken sins of their ancestors.

Then came another loud bang, this one even more forceful, this time from one of the doors downstairs.

Ernesto stood up, now genuinely worried.

"I think someone may have actually gotten in," he said, realizing that in the earlier commotion, he had forgotten to lock the door.

But before he could move, Dagoberto stopped him.

"Ask it if it was the ghost of our colonial ancestors," he said quietly.

Dagoberto had always been uneasy about his family's past.

This took Ernesto by surprise.

And because he still felt shaken, and guilty, about what had been revealed earlier about Dagoberto's sister, he asked the question quickly, almost absentmindedly:

"Was that the ghost of people from the colonial times here in the pharmacy?" Ernesto asked.

The planchette creepily glided toward **No**, then continued to move, letter by letter, to spell something out.

E-V-I-L-D-E-A-D

It took them a few seconds to figure it out, trying at first to read it as one word. But once they wrote it down, the meaning became clear.

Suddenly, three loud bangs echoed through the building, this time sounding like something heavy being dragged across the stairs.

Ernesto shot up and rushed to the landing, with Daniel and Dagoberto right behind him.

As he reached the space just before the staircase, a wave of dread crashed over him like a panic attack. His breath shortened. His skin went cold.

He looked down toward the base of the stairs, and froze.

There, on the marble floor, was what appeared to be a decayed and deformed human figure, midway through decomposition, pulling itself along as if unable to walk. It made low, garbled sounds, its tongue seemingly missing, incapable of forming intelligible words. It wore tattered rags and was shackled in iron restraints with long, rusted chains that clanked against the floor as it slithered snake-like across the tiles.

Its eyes shone with malevolence, full of perverse, evil intent.

The friends stood paralyzed.

But Dagoberto snapped them out of their trance with a firm slap on the shoulder and a warning: "*Hide!* It's trying to reach us!"

They ran, ducking into the loft above the second floor. Panicked and unsure what to do, they huddled there, surrounded by porcelain vases and glass containers from the museum's collection. Then Dagoberto remembered a phrase from one of the conference lectures, something a spiritist had repeated over and over:

"*Luz y Progreso. En el nombre del Señor. Amén!*"

He began chanting it.

Meanwhile, the chains banged louder and louder in the stairwell, drawing closer with each passing second.

By the tenth repetition of the phrase, the noise stopped.

Still, none of them dared to go check. They remained huddled in the loft, porcelain vases in hand, ready to throw them as projectiles if needed.

Ten minutes passed. Silence.

Finally, Ernesto snapped out of it. He looked at Daniel and Dagoberto and scolded them: "You can't handle antiques like that!"

They all got up and cautiously descended the stairs together.

Nothing was there.

Relieved but shaken, they went to retrieve the Ouija board and were about to pack it up when Dagoberto said:

"We need to ask permission to close the session."

"Are you crazy? You want *more* of this?" said Daniel.

"Let's just do it. Just in case. Put your hand on the planchette with mine, and let's ask," said Ernesto.

The friends did it, they placed their hands on the planchette one final time and asked for permission to close the session.

The planchette moved to **Yes**.

They gathered their things and made their way downstairs to leave the museum. As they descended, Ernesto felt more alive than he had in years. A surge of energy pulsed through him. He mentioned his excitement, half-sharing, half-testing his friends to see how they'd respond.

Both Daniel and Dagoberto admitted that nothing good had come from the experience, that they didn't want to do anything like it ever again. But they told Ernesto they respected him if he felt differently.

Ernesto nodded. "I do want to. You're my friends... I have no one else."

They both apologized but excused themselves, saying they couldn't do this again.

When they reached the museum door, Daniel and Dagoberto saw the conflicting look on Ernesto's face, he was both excited and disappointed. Excited by the experience but saddened that he wouldn't be able to share it again with them.

Daniel, standing at the door, turned to him and said quietly, "I'm sorry." He hugged Ernesto, then hugged Dagoberto, and left without looking back.

Dagoberto also said goodbye and began walking home. But when he was about a hundred meters away, just as Ernesto was closing the door, he turned back. Standing beneath the chemist's lantern in the dense morning fog, he called out:

"You know, my friend... I think you're crazy if you want to keep doing this. But I can see something's eating at you. So, to thank you for asking about my sister..."

"Yes, sorry about that," Ernesto interjected.

Dagoberto waved him off with a flick of the hand.

"There's an upcoming lecture next week, after Holy Week. A renowned psychiatrist and his daughter are presenting on past life regressions. Might be of interest to you. The tickets are sold out, but I've got a spare. Neither my wife nor the kids are into this kind of stuff."

"Yes. That would be great. Thank you!" said Ernesto, a spark returning to his eyes.

Dagoberto walked back and gave him a hug. "Don't forget to turn off the lantern," he reminded.

Ernesto nodded. Dagoberto disappeared into the thick fog, which was so dense he couldn't see more than a hundred meters ahead.

Ernesto stood in the doorway for a moment, then turned off the lantern and locked the door.

As he walked away, he muttered to himself, over and over, half-whispering, half-proclaiming:

"Yes… Yes. I want more. This is what I need. This is what my soul needs. I *knew* it, not that monotonous life I've been leading."

~

The night before the lecture, Ernesto had barely slept. The past week had felt like an eternity, and he was eagerly anticipating this new experience. He had been feeling this way more and more lately, detached, distracted, and it had even led to arguments with his fiancée over his absent-mindedness.

In fact, that morning, they had a rough argument, one that teetered on the brink of a breakup. She told him she would be visiting her parents that week. It had been a long time since she'd seen them, and, she said, they needed a break from each other, to figure out whether they truly wanted to get married and spend the rest of their lives together.

Instead of jolting him awake to the reality of his crumbling personal life, her words only deepened the pull of his recent experience. He remembered the Ouija board's message clearly: he wouldn't marry Sonia, but someone with the initials **M.R.**, not Sonia's initials.

He wasn't blind to the possibility that this could be a kind of self-fulfilling prophecy. But still, he felt as though he were under a spell, drawn along by something greater.

"Honestly," he said aloud, "I don't even care."

And so, Ernesto went to work. Later, during lunch, as had become customary, he left for the lecture at the library.

His friend Dagoberto greeted him warmly at the entrance, handed him the ticket, and quickly excused himself. He explained that he needed to focus on a lot of behind-the-scenes work for the event, as the guest speaker was a high-profile figure. Ernesto nodded in understanding, and Dagoberto brought his hands together in a praying gesture to say thank you before disappearing inside.

Ernesto handed his ticket to the attendant and entered the lecture hall.

It was already packed. He barely managed to find a seat, one of the last, in an uncomfortable section toward the back. It wasn't ideal, but he didn't care.

After about twenty minutes, and some commotion outside the room, the speakers finally entered: an elderly white man with a full head of white hair, accompanied by his much younger, brunette daughter.

Applause erupted. Some visitors even cried out emotionally.

Ernesto didn't recognize the man, but based on the reaction, it was clear he was a respected figure in this spiritual community, just as Dagoberto had said.

He settled in to listen.

The speaker began by introducing his book and discussing his work. Ernesto followed along and grasped the gist of it, but he wasn't convinced.

"*Past life regression through a kind of hypnotism?*" he thought. "*That sounds like a load of crap to me.*"

Then, after a pause, he added mentally, "*Although... I've never tested whether I could be hypnotized or not. That could be fun.*"

Ernesto betrayed his deepest desire, he wanted to experiment, to try, to experience. He wanted to live and breathe change, transformation, and even chaos. He felt he had peaked too early and was now stagnant, trapped. And so he craved something new, even if it meant destruction.

After a short talk, which felt immensely long and somewhat boring to Ernesto, who had barely listened, he drifted into daydreams about traveling to Europe and visiting the Notre-Dame Cathedral. It wasn't until the end of the talk that the speakers announced they would be leading a mass past life regression session with the entire audience.

The room erupted in unanimous cheers, jolting Ernesto from his reverie.

He followed the speakers' instructions, closing his eyes and breathing in rhythm with their words, but at first, he experienced nothing. His mind continued to chatter in disconnected fragments: monologues, reactions, conversations, memories from earlier that day and the week before. It spiraled, restless and repetitive.

Eventually, he arrived at the memory of that morning's argument with Sonia, a memory he didn't want to face. He resisted it, circling it mentally like a wound he didn't want to touch.

Then, almost like a whisper from somewhere deep inside, he heard himself say:

"Let go."

And he did.

He fell into a heavy, enveloping state. External stimuli vanished. The room, the sounds, the murmurs, all gone. What remained was darkness and utter silence.

Then, slowly, fragments began to appear, shifting shapes like a kaleidoscope. But these weren't his memories. They weren't scenes he had ever lived or seen. And yet, somehow, they felt familiar. He didn't recognize them, but he felt integrated within them. Gradually, the kaleidoscopic fragments gave way to fully formed visions.

He found himself standing in an unfamiliar place. The surroundings looked like something out of the pictures he had seen of ancient Rome or Greece, the way people dressed, the architecture, the colors of the sky.

He looked up.

In front of him rose a massive colonnaded structure. He was standing beneath its towering columns, gazing at the inscription carved into the upper portion of its stone façade.

ΓΝΩΘΙ ΣΕΑΥΤΟΝ ΜΗΔΕΝ ΑΓΑΝ ΕΓΓΥΑ ΠΑΡΑ Δ' ΑΤΑ

He saw himself bow in reflection as he entered the building and was greeted by an older man. They spoke in a language Ernesto didn't consciously recognize, yet he understood every word.

The man was scolding him for being late and told him to reflect on the third maxim:

ΕΓΓΥΑ ΠΑΡΑ Δ᾽ ΑΤΑ
("Make a pledge and mischief is near.")

As a priest in training of Apollo, the man said, Ernesto was expected to uphold a higher standard.

Then he asked Ernesto to recite the role of divination and prophecy.

Ernesto was surprised to hear the words rise from his own mouth: That divination was the art of re-tracing or re-collecting, a sacred process of freeing the soul from its mortal prison. This stood in opposition to the re-binding forces of the malevolent.

Hence, the importance of the first maxim:

ΓΝΩΘΙ ΣΕΑΥΤΟΝ
("Know thyself.")

He understood now: the ethics of self-formation and self-care, through ritual, mentorship, introspection, and bodily discipline, formed the fundamental path to spiritual self-knowledge. Through this ethical preparation, one became worthy of truth, not through intellect or reason alone, but through a full transformation of being.

The elder priest then directed him to look at the sky.
"Trace where the planets are transiting today," he commanded. "It is essential you retain this skill and are able to map it correctly. And when you cannot, use the tool that keeps track of it."

Then the vision began to dissolve.

The scene disintegrated, and slowly, through the same process, another vision emerged.

This time, Ernesto found himself in a large, dark building entrance. He and others around him wore robes resembling those often depicted in Egyptian hieroglyphs.

He stepped outside and saw a temple under construction.

Along its outer wall, the following hieroglyphs were being carved:

However, he was quickly turned around by an echoing voice that called his name:

"Ernesto..."

He was startled, almost pulled out of the trance.

Who could possibly be calling him by name *here*?

He turned back toward the building's interior, as if drawn by a magnetic pull, and found himself moving deeper, into a shadowed room.

There, in the dim glow, sat a figure.

It spoke to him in Spanish and English, the languages Ernesto understood.

He was stunned.

"Who are you?" asked Ernesto.

"I am the force that guides you," the figure said. "I am your spiritual source and foundation. We have been together for millennia. Do you not recognize me?"

Ernesto fell silent, then asked again, more carefully:

"Who... are you?"

"I am known to you by many names," the being replied. "First, in the Atlantean age, do you remember your time there?"

"I've had dreams," Ernesto admitted, "of living in a city beneath the ocean... a place with advanced technology and a refined culture. If that's what you mean?"

"Yes. Those were glimpses I illuminated for you, preparations for this day. In that life, you knew me as Hermes Trismegistus, and you served as one of my chief priests."

The figure then reached to one of the torches on the wall and pulled it closer, revealing more of his form.

"Later, you knew me in Egypt, as you see me now," he continued. "I was called Thoth... but made immortal, mummified and preserved by Osiris himself, even beyond the end of Egypt."

Ernesto stared. The being did, indeed, resemble a mummy, covered in fine, alternating green and yellow wrappings. And yet, beneath the bandages, he looked vibrant and strong. Youthful. Vital. He sat in lotus position, holding palm nuts in his hands, which he gently gestured toward Ernesto with a soft smile.

Surrounding him were objects, familiar ones. Chains, astrology charts, palm nuts, coins, cards... a full array of oracles. Ernesto's eyes landed on the divining chain and the astrological charts.

"Ah," the figure said knowingly. "Those look familiar to you in this incarnation, don't they?"

Ernesto nodded.

"Yes," the being continued. "These are the latest forms, tools developed in my honor, and ones I have blessed. You know me also as Apollo... and more recently, as Ọ̀rúnmìlà."

He leaned forward slightly.

"Would you like me to use them to divine your destiny? To help you re-trace and re-collect who you truly are?"

Ernesto was taken aback by the question, though he smiled faintly.

It was the first time he had really looked at the being's face. He noticed now that when he spoke, his lips barely moved, as though he were whispering truths that didn't need to be voiced loudly.

"What's the matter?" the figure asked. "Didn't you come to discover why you've been feeling empty? Confused?"

"Yes," Ernesto answered, in a soft, almost childlike tone.

"Well then," the being said gently, "let me show you."

He lifted a scroll and unrolled it.

"Here is your birth chart. You, see? You were born under the gaze of Saturn:"[1]

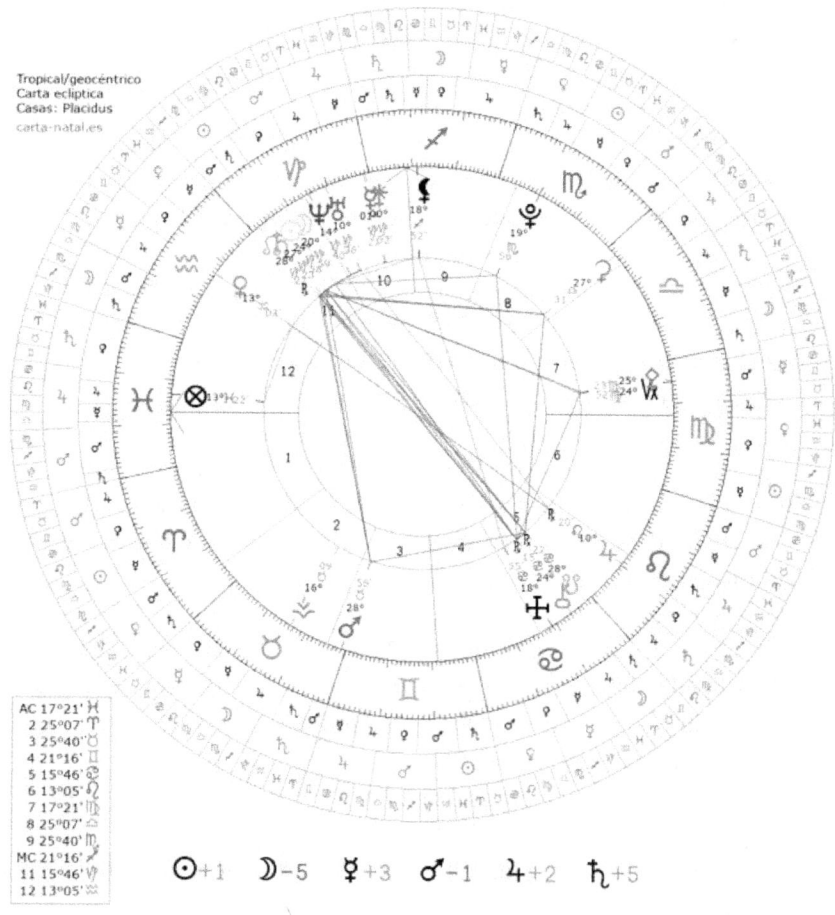

Tropical/geocéntrico
Carta eclíptica
Casas: Placidus
carta-natal.es

AC 17°21' ♓
2 25°07' ♈
3 25°40' ♉
4 21°16' ♊
5 15°46' ♋
6 13°05' ♌
7 17°21' ♍
8 25°07' ♎
9 25°40' ♏
MC 21°16' ♐
11 15°46' ♑
12 13°05' ♒

☉+1   ☽−5   ☿+3   ♂−1   ♃+2   ♄+5

"From him you have come... and to him you will return, where you will be judged by the judges who stand at those gates..."

1. *I extend my heartfelt thanks to Sylvia de Ayala, owner and developer of carta-natal.es, for generously granting me permission to use the natal chart generated through her remarkable software on the website.*

"Do you understand now?" the being asked. "You cannot escape your destiny. You have been living the life programmed for you *in the world*, not *in heaven*, a life designed to keep you bounded and blinded to eternal reality.

"Existence is the identity of God, and we are its fractal mirror image.

"It is time for you to accept your destiny. You must continue my labor, as you now know me: Ọrúnmìlà. You must mature into a babalawo, *Odi Owonrin*.

+

I

0

0

I

"You represent the balance between order, silence, structure, confinement, containment, gestation, privacy, boundaries, repression, and things hidden or sealed, and instability, motion, change, the unexpected, speech, rhythm, volatility, revolution, and revelation. "You are the eye in the center of the hurricane and the tornado. The voice of wisdom and order amidst chaos and folly. The dynamic interplay between Saturn and Uranus, or Obàtálá and Èṣù, light and dark.

"And to Him must you return, having stabilized what is volatile and secured what is vulnerable."

A resonant bell sound echoed through the chamber as Ọrúnmìlà smiled softly.

Ernesto *snapped* out of the trance, as if thrown backward in reverse.

Dagoberto, who had been watching him the entire time during the meditation, saw his body jolt with a full hypnic jerk. He couldn't help but laugh.

It was the first sound Ernesto heard as he came back to the room, and he recognized that laugh anywhere. It made him smile.

Dagoberto came over and gently touched his shoulder.

"You good, man?" he asked.

How could Ernesto possibly explain what he had just seen, just *felt*?

So instead, he simply said:

"How long was I out? I sure needed a nap today. Hahaha."

Dagoberto laughed too.

Then, with a touch of sincerity and curiosity, he asked, "Did you see anything? Learn anything?"

Ernesto nodded slowly.

"Yes," he said. "I saw myself... and learned that which I *am*."

A Canon of Eleven Voices

Setting:

Early winter or late fall. A campfire on the outskirts of Atlanta, Georgia. The campfire is managed and owned by the King Center. About 40 yards (ca. 37 m) from the cabin, where the campfire is, our scholars and activists sit around a medium to high fire, placed in the middle of a makeshift circle. The circle, centered on a pile of logs, is made of camp chairs and blankets that are used for seating or lying down by each of the characters in this play. The fire lights their faces in a warm but subdued way, giving greater gravitas to facial expressions, while also leading to some difficulty interpreting their facial expressions. A lake sits to the left of the campfire at the opposite end of the Cabin, which reflects a crescent moon and a mountain with a small snow cap.

Stage:

Left of the field of vision-Mountains, lake
   Center of field of vision: Campfire, logs, blankets, chairs and main personas of the story
   Right of field of vision: Two -story cabin with floodlights dimly lighting up to about 32 yards (ca. 29 m) before the backs of characters to the right of the campfire

Characters:

1. Martin Luther King Jr.

2. Malcom X

3. W. E. B. Du Bois

4. E. Franklin Frazier.

5. Melville Herskovits

6. Sid Mintz

7. Sally Price

8. Richard Price

9. N. Fadeke Castor.

10. Christina Sharpe

11. Manning Marable

> "But the past does not exist independently from the present. Indeed, the past is only past because there is a present, just as I can point to something over there only because I am here. But nothing is inherently over there or here. In that sense, the past has no content. The past—or, more accurately, pastness—is a position. Thus, in no way can we identify the past as past."[1]
>
> —Michel-Rolph Trouillot, Silencing the Past: Power and the Production of History

---

1. Trouillot, *Silencing the Past*, 15.

Part I: The Encounter

(Fire crackling)

Martin Luther King Jr: (Just finished praying or come off deep contemplation) Thank you for coming tonight brothers and sisters. I am honored to be in your presence and for you to put aside your differences in the name of the Black future.

— All share pleasantries, more or less in unison.

Martin Luther King Jr.: As the grandfather of African American studies and the most senior person here, I would like to cede first thoughts to Dr. Du Bois. Please lead our evening Dr. Du Bois.

W. E. B. Du Bois: Thank you, thank you, Dr. King. I am honored to be here as well and really appreciate the time and effort you have put into actively catering to all our needs. Our own talented 11th. (Du Bois allows a soft smile to show on his face).

Malcom X: Talented 11th?! Brother, brother. The Black future is not dependent on intellectualism, but on the ground activism and militarism. What did the talented 10th accomplish, but to alienate those brothers and sisters whose material conditions did not mirror your bourgeois reality? And where is Marcus Garvey? Why was he not invited today? Did he not merit inclusion in your so-called talented 10th?

Sally Price: And women!

Christina Sharpe: Preach it girl! Absolutely!

Martin Luther King Jr.: One moment. One moment, please. Brothers and sisters, we are not here today to actively sabotage and to break each other down. It is the White men's prerogative to do so. Rather, I would like for us to focus on actual points of interest, and commonality. In particular, I would like for us to focus on four main points that still fester in this *colonial present*. First, I would like for us to discuss the origins of African American culture. Secondly, I would like to approach a definition of Blackness. Thirdly,

I think we should focus on the relationship between activism and scholarship.

Malcom X: Amen, brother.

Martin Luther King Jr.: (Small pause) Fourth, I would like to conclude by encouraging all of us to think about the best way for us to move forward.

— The conversation is halted by the camp's servers who bring some marshmallows and chocolate as well as drinks (alcoholic and non-alcoholic) for the guests to enjoy. This changes the energy of the conversation and the tension is replaced by more pleasant exchanges between the quests.

Part II: The Realization

— Some time has passed, and the tense exchanges seem now like water under the bridge. The quests are sitting around the fire once more and slowly get into a more somber mood.

Melville Herskovits: If I am allowed a moment, ladies and gentlemen. I would like to get back to reflections Dr. King, and to start the conversation on your first point. After all, I am the pioneer in the field of African American studies and tradition. Before me, the field was a perfect vacuum (Mintz, 1990, p. ix). Hence, I do not agree with your statement Dr. King, about Dr. Du Bois being the grandfather of African American studies.

W.E. B. Du Bois: Here we go again with the slander and your attempts at undermining me.

Melville Herskovits: I am just stating the obvious. My work *The Myth of the Negro Past* is the foremost representative of Afrocentrism, according to other scholars (Herskovits at the Heart of Blackness.2009). Overall, my position is that the origins of African American culture among contemporary Afro-Americans represent a survival of African customs, beliefs, and practices. They represent survivals that have stood the test of radical influences by other cultures. Nonetheless, these survivals do demonstrate the syncretic nature of African American culture, whose highly creolized nature leads to a distinction between race and culture. This is exemplified by the maroon slaves who made a life for themselves in the wilderness of Latin America and Haiti (Mintz, 1990, p. xii-xv).

Christina Sharpe: So, you make no room for the afterlives of slavery? How about the domination and oppression of White hegemony that keeps black folk in a perpetual state of precarity? We live in the *wake* of colonialism, do we not? (Sharpe, 2016, p.12 & 17)

Sidney Mintz: If I may, Dr. Herskovits.

Melville Herskovits: Please (assents with a hand gesture for her to continue).

Sidney Mintz: I think his work does, but its importance is secondary to the strength and endurance of culture and its survivals (Mintz, 1990, p. xii-xx).

N. Fadeke Castor: I believe so as well! And not only is this true, but also the transnational pathways of spiritual citizenship have also demonstrated that African and African American culture are more deeply linked than ever. African American identity is found in the return to and reclaim of African indigenous beliefs and practices (Castor, 2017, p. 5–7)

Malcom X: Is that so? African Americans, Hispanics, and Africans are the true children of Israel; and Islam is the true religion. We have been dominated by the white poison of Christianity and kept by the power of Satan in these idolatrize. Pure *shirk*.

N. Fadeke Castor: Those are very strong words Malcom. I think they reflect the brainwashing of foreign Abrahamic cultures and religions on Black bodies. This is why the only path forward is by joining with the original African beliefs and practices and to strengthen the transnational ties with our brothers and sisters.

Sally Price: One must be careful about making such grand statements about the continuations and transatlantic/transnational pathways and survivals of African culture in the New World. These moments of discovery and realization need to be grounded, and their uniqueness should be emphasized. The emergence of creole traditions often reflects deeply syncretic variations and inventions that mark a break with the past. Or at least seem to make a new moment of emergence and creation that no longer signifies or reflects the past (Price and Price, p. 16–23).

Martin Luther King Jr.: It does not matter color, creed or culture. We are all children of God and African American culture is the spiritual essence of America.

— Some agree while others remain silent. At this point, a large proportion of the guests just demonstrate their desire to move along in the discussion. Not all are interested in the point or direction of the conversation.

Part III: Black is...Black ain't

— At this stage, in the evening, guests have already enjoyed the refreshment and food, and a feeling of solidarity has started to replace the original tensions of their encounters. Besides this, the party inside the cabin has also started playing some music. In particular, the party is playing Black music and the guests begin to reflect and discuss this paradox in the United States of America.

W. E B. Du Bois: You know... the other day I was watching a documentary titled *Black is..... Black ain't*, where the reality of the politics of struggle and the complexity of African American identity was underscored by the director, Marlon Troy Riggs (Riggs, 1995). This reminded me of my fieldwork in Philadelphia and of the importance of empirical data for deciphering the complexity of Black reality in America, as constituted by the intersectionality of multiple variables constituting the Black experience (Hancock, 2005, p. 1–3).

Melville Herskovits: I would add that this intersectionality is the essence of syncretism. For example, this music is a mix of African beats and percussive instruments with European vocals and tradition of music, homegrown on American soil.

W. E. B. Du Bois: It is the new N++++ spirituals. It reflects the inner city and the politics of struggle of Black identity and culture (Massiah, 1996).

Christine Sharpe: Not only that, but it also reflects the perpetual *wake consciousness* of Black America. The violence, precarity and overall experience of having to defend the dead, while trying to escape a situation that has no escape but through community support. The Black experience is marked by invented characterizations and experiences. It is the subjectification of the Black consciousness and experience in terms of normalization of pain and precarity. This is why *wake work* needs to be activated at the community level. It is the only path forward through the wake of colonization and recolonization of globalization (Sharpe, 2016, p.14–16 & 20–24).

Malcom X: Black is heritage....black ain't shame, brothers, and sisters.

— They all agree on this.

Part IV: It Takes a Village.

Manning Marble: This was an excellent epitaph, Malcom. Thank you for synthesizing our thoughts on this matter. However, thinking a bit more about Christine last point on the role of the community and our previous conversation on the intellectualism and activism, I would like to go back to it now. I would like to talk about Dr. King's third point of discussion, related to this. It is my opinion that for Black folks to be able to transform their material conditions, a point you have brought up in this conversation before Dr. Du Bois, we need to combine scholarly research with activism. It is impossible to contest and transform the institutionalized system of oppression and racism through armchair scholarship. Black folks and Black communities also need active presence and community engagement through activism. However, that activism is only realized through a change of consciousness, which is what scholarly research does (Marable, 2000, p. 2–4).

E. Franklin Frazier: This is an excellent point Manning; one that has echoes in my own work as found in *Nation and Opportunity*. The scholar's misunderstanding of action and activism has led to a rift between the needs of African Americans in the U.S. Moreover, it also touches on Malcom's point about Marcus Garvey. Why isn't he here? As I mentioned before "*The Work carried out by [the NAACP] ... has never attracted the crowd" and the leadership of Dr. Du Bois has been too intellectual to satisfy the mob*" (as quoted in; Matsumoto, 2005, p. 57–58).

Christine Sharpe: All this questioning about Garvey is starting to remind me of *Waiting for Godot* (Beckett, 2006).
— All look at each other in perplexity of Sharpe's statement.

Christine Sharpe: Never mind that.
— Silence. About 2 long minutes pass, in which time the sipping of chocolate and the crackling of the fire gets amplified by the deafening silence.

N. Fadeke Castor: Ubuntu.

W. E. B Du Bois: What?

N. Fadeke Castor: It is an African philosophy that emphasizes being and identity of individuals through others. In other words, it conveys the formation of an identity through the spirit of solidarity of a community that is encapsulated in the phrase "*ubuntu ngumuntu ngabantu* (I am because of who we all are)" (Mugumbate, 2013, p. 81).
   — Some nod while others verbally express their agreement with this African philosophy.

Martin Luther King Jr.: Brothers and sisters. Thank you for this, must wonderful evening. As the night becomes long and weary, and the winter evening gives way to a spring of rebirth, please reflect of Christine's call for defending the dead. Please remember that modernity stands on the shoulders of giants, but also on the bodies of Black and Brown peoples which it sacrificed in the name of progress and enlightenment. So, do not forget your history, do not forget your suffering, but most importantly, do not forget your humanity and your love. "Darkness cannot drive out darkness, only light can do that. Hate cannot drive out hate, only love can do that." (King Jr, 1964, p.45).

GOD

Photo by David Eucaristia on Pexels.com

GOD

D

ὁ θεός E יהוה

U

S

From thyself emanated all,
And with just a word was
Creation born. The vibration
Of its echoes still lives in matter

And eternal in time it rattles,
While Light and darkness battle
For what matters most,
Your soul to be. Grace shined

Down, darkness transformed.
Father, Son and Holy Spirit
As the primacy of existence

From which reality is born.
And thus emanated all
Creation, with your word, Be.

Bibliography

Beckett, Samuel. (2006). *Waiting for Godot*. London: Faber And Faber.

Castor, N. Fadeke. (2017). *Spiritual Citizenship: Transnational Pathways from Black Power to Ifá in Trinidad*. Durham: Duke University Press.

Hancock, Ange-Marie .(2005). "W.E.B. Du Bois: Intellectual Forefather of Intersectionality?" *Souls* 7, no. 3–4: 74–84. https://doi.org/10.1080/10999940500265508.

Herskovits at the Heart of Blackness. Films On Demand. 2009. Accessed October 23, 2023. https://digital.films.com/PortalPlaylists.aspx?wID=107350&xtid=49778.

King Jr., Martin Luther. *Strength to Love*. Pocket, 1964.

Marable, M. (2005). Reconstructing the Radical Du Bois. *Souls*, 7(3–4), 1–25. Retrieved from http://www.tandfonline.com/doi/abs/10.1080/10999940500265391

———. (2000). Introduction. *Dispatches from the Ebony Tower: Intellectuals Confront the African-American Experience* (pp. 1–28). New York: Columbia University Press.

Massiah, Louis. (1996). W.E.B. Du Bois: A Biography in Four Voices. California Newsreel. https://video.alexanderstreet.com/watch/w-e-b-du-bois-a-biography-in-4-voices.

Matsumoto, M. (2005). E. Franklin Frazier on W.E.B. Du Bois: Sociologist, critic, and friend. *Souls*, 7(3–4), 55–71. doi:10.1080/10999940500265458

Milton, John. *Paradise Lost*. Book I. In *The Complete Poetical Works of John Milton*, edited by Henry W. Boynton. Boston: Houghton Mifflin, 1909.

Mintz, S. W. (1990). Introduction. In M. Herskovits (Ed.), *The Myth of the Negro Past* (pp. ix–xxii). Boston: Beacon. Retrieved from http://www.springerlink.com/index/M368G660J3244576.pdf

Mugumbate, J. & Nyanguru, A. (2013). Exploring African philosophy: The Value of Ubuntu in Social Work. African Journal of Social Work, 3 (1), 82–100.

Plotinus. *The Six Enneads*. Translated by Stephen MacKenna and B. S. Page. London: Medici Society, 1917.

Price, R., & Price, S. (2003). *The Root of Roots, or, How Afro-American Anthropology Got its Start*. Chicago: Prickly Paradigm. Retrieved from http://evols.library.manoa.hawaii.edu/handle/10524/1559

Riggs, Marlon T. (1995). Black Is, Black Ain't. San Fransisco, CA: California Newsreel.

Bibliography

Sharpe, Christina Elizabeth. (2016). *In the Wake: On Blackness and Being.* Durham: Duke University Press.

Trouillot, M.-R. and Carby, H.V. (2015) *Silencing the Past: Power and the Production of History.* Boston: Beacon.